I0621553

The Wizard of Black Hollow

Copyright 2020 by Samantha Allard

978-1-68361-501-9Print ISBN: 978-1-68361-501-9

Cover art by Fantasia Frog Designs

Published by Decadent Publishing Company, LLC

Look for us online at:

www.decadentpublishing.com

When a dragon horrifically murders his companions, the wizard Yosef quits his life as an adventurer. Instead of spells, he conjures sweet cakes and breads in his bakery. Instead of treasure, he opts for coin. And instead of magical shields, he dons a grouchy mantle to avoid any and all personal connections. He is quite happy never to go on an adventure again.

The daughter of a dragon and a human man, Ayako attracts trouble like a magnet. A run-in with an orc leads her to the wizard Yosef. Her empathic ability reveals there's more to this man than his grumpy outer shell.

He wants to keep his previous life a secret. She longs for a life without the complication of being half dragon. Unfortunately, trouble isn't far behind, and they both need to face their pasts if they hope to have a future.

Thank you for taking the time to read 'The Wizard of Black Hollow.'

Yosef was the creation of one of my players in a roleplaying game I ran. With his permission, I decided to write what happened next to him after the campaign ended. I plucked him out of that world and placed him into a new one.

Ayako is a completely new character but one I fell in love with quickly. I'm looking forward to seeing how she grows in future stories.

If you'd like to talk to me about this or any of my other stories, I can be found at samanthaallard@hotmail.co.uk

Dedication

To the friends who helped to inspire this story. To the family who give me, mostly, uninterrupted writing time. To the readers who make me strive to be better.

The Wizard of Black Hollow
Spells and Scales Book 1

by

Samantha Allard

Prologue

Yosef Corinson couldn't be described as a reckless man. He put great thought into everything he did, which was why his travelling band of adventurers, the Mockery, were going to die today. The windy, nature-created corridors made a quick getaway out of the question. They were marching into a kill box. Having voiced his concerns, he'd prepared his spells accordingly for the day.

"Are you alright, boy?"

"I wish you would stop calling me that. I'm older than you." He glared over his shoulder at Grogswald. The elderly goblin, who used his staff as a makeshift walking stick, smiled up at him—an interesting sight coming from a goblin whose teeth didn't all seem to fit into his mouth. If he'd meant to be reassuring, he fell short of the mark.

"Why are you more worked up than usual?"

Polgrund and Dust hurried off in front of them, and farther in front of them was Sticky. The halfling had always suffered a case of the "light fingers," but he was quick on his feet, barely making a sound. The perfect person to lead the charge, Sticky would check to see if the Golden Dawn was indeed asleep. It would be up to him to grab the scales the adventurers had been hired to procure, the key ingredient to a potion.

"I was looking forward to growing old."

"You're being dramatic. We've handled worse things."

"Unless we've battled a dragon at some point and I've forgotten, I beg to differ." He muttered under his breath.

There was the barest hint of movement in front of them. Polgrund and Dust came to a halt as Sticky stepped out of the shadows. "Got about twenty feet before we hit its lair. Wizard Branch was right, it's fast asleep. Fairly sure I can get in there, grab the scales, and get out without being noticed."

"And what happens if he wakes?" They might have all been whispering, but Yosef doubted it made much of a difference.

"Wizard Branch said it slept during the day. We'll be fine," Dust said from his place at the front.

"We need those scales, or people are going to die. I would prefer he didn't wake, but we're not leaving without those scales," Gru spoke up from behind them, another goblin but completely different from

Grogswald. His scales, a deep, dark red, helped him blend into the shadows. His manner of speech also set him apart, due to his upbringing with elves.

Gru strolled past them, and Yosef shared a look with Grogswald. The other goblin raised his hand, preventing him from joining the rest of the party. They stopped a few feet away.

The elderly goblin gave him a serious stare. "You've got your teleportation spell ready, haven't you, boy?"

"Always, but you know I can't take anyone with me. If it all goes to hell, then we're going to be stuck." A talented wizard with a vast range of spells he might have been, but there was still plenty of things to learn. A few more months and he might be powerful enough to take someone with him when he jumped. That wouldn't help them now.

"If that happens, if it all goes wrong, we'll get the scales to you and you need to get out."

He shook his head before the goblin even finished speaking. "That's insane. I'm not leaving any of you behind."

"We've discussed this already," Polgrund spoke up. The human Paladin always carried a small cage on his back. An odd style choice but he could transport his

3

bounty more easily when he finally caught up with them. Polgrund could also use the cage to transport treasure, which was probably why he had insisted on bringing it along. Dragons hoarded gold, and Polgrund made no secret of his desire for it.

Yosef glanced around at them, noting how some couldn't meet his gaze. "When did you have this discussion?"

"When you were talking to the Wizard Branch. Hopefully, it won't come to that. It's the worst-case scenario." Dust crossed his arms. "We all want to leave this place alive, and maybe we'll be lucky. But if we're not? One of us needs to get out of here with the scales. Might as well be you."

He turned his focus on Grogswald, not hiding the incredulous feeling which swept over him. "And what about Elsbeth?" The goblin's granddaughter made Yosef promise her grandfather would survive the encounter. She promised to inflict her axe on him, which left him in little doubt she would follow through on it.

The goblin smiled, sadly. "I can't teleport, kid. That would be you."

He and Grogswald stayed by the cave entrance, which opened into a wide space with an enormous hole at the very top, letting in beams of sunlight. The jagged stone walls possessed no easy handholds. In the centre of the space sat a large pile of gold pieces and jewels, but atop that the Golden Dawn lay asleep. He tried to judge the size of the dragon, with the beast curled up as it was, he could only hazard a guess. Twenty-four feet long perhaps? Its large head was partially hidden underneath a pile of gold like a puppy that had buried its head under its favourite blanket. A large, scaly puppy with a wicked set of sharp teeth.

Swords drawn, Polgrund and Dust positioned themselves on either side of the dragon, keeping their distance but still prepared. Gru stood facing the beast, his staff poised and ready for anything. Yosef couldn't shake the looming sense of doom which grew in the pit of his stomach.

Sticky carefully moved closer to the sleeping form. They had already decided he would need to circle the beast, checking the floor for any loose scales which had fallen off. Much easier to take than ones still attached to the dragon. Sticky disappeared behind the great beast, and he held his breath until the halfling reappeared. He raised a heavy pouch high into the air and gave them all a thumbs-up. Yosef let out the breath he'd held and glanced back at the Golden

Dawn—whose eyes were open.

"It's awake!"

The beast raised up on its hind legs, spreading out his wings and filling the entire cave. Sticky, in the middle of sneaking back to them, was dwarfed by its large frame. The Golden Dawn swivelled its head and snapped forward, grabbing the halfling across the torso. Sticky swung the pouch in Polgrund's direction as he screamed in pain and then nothing. The dragon flung their comrade into the corner then twisted, on the sudden movement of Polgrund drawing its attention. The paladin had turned, dashing toward the entrance. The beast lashed out with its claw, and, for a second, he thought the large creature missed. But then Polgrund fell backwards, throwing the pouch, and blindly swung his sword. Dust dashed towards the struggling pair—a pointless exercise in bravery.

Yosef conjured an energy ball, pulling together the ethereal threads making up the magical world, until they formed a glowing blue orb. Though not physical, the sphere weighed about a quarter stone. He moved both hands back to his hip before thrusting them forward. The ball of energy flew, crackling with magic until it hit the hind of the beast. The dragon roared in fury, the sound bouncing off the walls. He slammed his

6

hands over his ears, noticing Grogswald doing the same. Hard to focus on casting when a person couldn't think.

Yosef grabbed Grogswald's shoulder and yelled, "We need spells. Anything to slow it down. Buy the others some time."

Gru ran past them. The small Goblin jammed the bottom of his staff into the ground, shouting out a word that was drowned out by the dragon's roar. Tendrils of trees burst through the ground, cracking the stone beneath the beast, and wrapped themselves around the large form, holding the dragon in place. Gru grinned over his shoulder at them. "And you were worried this would prove too much for us?"

"Gru, watch out!" He watched in horror as the large dragon clawed into the goblin's back. Gru screamed out in obvious pain. Instinct kicked in, and Yosef darted forward to do something, anything to help, but the elderly goblin's hand on his wrist stopped him.

"You need to get out." Grogswald shoved the full pouch at him, and, due to his small size, hit his hip and not his chest. "I can buy you some time. Tell my granddaughter I died a hero and I love her."

"I'm not leaving you. Come with me."

The Wizard of Black Hollow

"Don't be stupid, kid. This is much more important than one life. Much more important than mine." The goblin faced the dragon which tore into Gru's twitching form. A steely determination lit in the old goblin's blue eyes, and he shrugged. "Who knows? Maybe he'll choke on me. Old meat is the toughest after all."

Chapter One

Two years later...

Nightmares plagued him. No, the word paled in comparison to the nightly reminders from his past. A nightmare signified something he could wake up from. A state of mind brought on by bad food or cheese, at least for others. These were memories. The day they fought the Golden Dawn and lost. He'd thought time and distance would help bring him some peace. It hadn't. The screams echoing in the cavern still haunted him. The yells of excruciating pain and his inability to help. The sound of the sharp teeth of an angry dragon cracking armour and tearing into flesh. The memory of that day never truly left him.

He closed his eyes, rubbing the bridge of his nose. He would have gladly lived without the knowledge that armour cracking sounded like a bird breaking a nut to get to the kernel inside. Gru's screams still haunted him to this day. He only survived because of the teleportation spell he kept as backup. One use. One person. A last resort if everything went to hell. The party had thrown the dragon scales to him for that very reason.

It hadn't been his idea to go up against a dragon. The beasts were dangerous, unpredictable because of their sheer intelligence and ruthlessness. The wizard Lucien Branch had hired the party to retrieve the scales needed for a healing potion. He had offered them a ridiculous sum of coin. The party was made up of dwarves and those who were swayed by shiny things. It was a lost cause to try and persuade them otherwise.

The Golden Dawn apparently slept heavily during the day. All they needed to do was sneak in, get some scales—the ones that had fallen off—and sneak back out. He would have refused the job because he wasn't stupid, nor did he need the money. He did, however, know the party wouldn't survive without him. They needed his skill with magic. Fighters and barbarians wouldn't get close enough to swing a sword before being rendered a charred mess.

A terrible idea, all in all.

And him being there hadn't kept his party alive.

He filled a basin with water from the large jug he'd prepared the night before, using the well behind Delectable Bites, his home and place of work. A few minutes of focusing on the basin with his hand on the base heated the water. A simple spell, a few words, and a gesture were all he needed. Magic required focus. If he lost control, he ran the risk of overheating the basin, making it explode. The spell was a balance, involving a sense of calm. Something he had in short supply.

He washed his face then ran his slender fingers through his hair, braiding and securing the strands with a band. The scent of freshly baked bread reached him in his room on the second floor of the bakery. He wished he'd been able to start his career as a baker instead of learning the skills of the magical world. He wouldn't have been introduced to the creatures who eventually became his companions. Then he wouldn't have these nightmares because he'd watched them die.

Yosef pulled his clothes on—simple beige trousers and a near-white collarless shirt. Over the top, he put on his black robes. The dark fabric wrapping his body gave him an almost sinister air, and if his attire dissuaded others from talking to him, all the better. He didn't have much contact with the customers at Delectable Bites anymore. The bakery had grown popular enough he'd hired staff, but he'd made a point not to make friends with any of them.

Hushed whispers reached him as he descended

the stairs. The layout of Delectable Bites was quite simple. Tables and chairs for people were currently all empty since they hadn't opened for the day. When they were busy, the laughter of children was a common sound. A large counter with a glass sheet protected the cakes and breads from grabby hands.

Nimue Lightfoot, an elf, ran the counter. Her long green hair, enhanced with charms, framed her face in soft waves. She certainly was a sight to see in a dress which matched the vibrant shade and a welcoming smile. An odd combination. Elves weren't known for their sunny disposition. Half of the men who walked through the door were probably there more for her smile than for the sweet goods sold. As long as they parted with their coin, he didn't care. He only wanted to be left alone to do what he always saw was his true purpose in life.

With a brisk nod to Nimue, he pushed open the door leading into the kitchen. Tamlic and Catlo glanced up from their area, both kneading different combinations of ingredients. The table wasn't a suitable height for gnomes, but he'd given them stools to use. Both worked hard, and gnomes were creative by nature, inventing machines that made most jobs easier. However, he preferred the old-school methods taught to him by his father.

Yosef checked over the work. The gnomes glanced up, and the conversation, in full flow before he walked in, came to a grinding halt. He kept a list of supplies they needed pinned to a board. There were ways and means to keep ingredients cool and fresh, but he preferred to buy fresh on the day, especially the milk Shepherd Miller delivered every morning.

He rolled up the long sleeves of his robe then retrieved a coin purse from its hook on the wall and a wicker basket from off the table by the exit. He pushed the door open and walked into the back alley. Thanks to the kitchen's open window, he didn't miss the fact that conversation had started again after the door swung shut behind him.

The small village of Black Hollow had decent foot traffic. Travellers came through here to get to the Baron's Keep to the west or the Silver Tree to the east—the place where the elves lived. The forge in the nearby Hammer and Sword's was always lit, creating a wall of heat leaving passers-by coated in a thin layer of sweat. How Godfrey managed to work in those conditions without passing out confounded him. Dwarves were made from hardy stuff.

Across the street, the halfling Jenae ran the

The Wizard of Black Hollow

Curative Potion and sold potions and healing components for any adventurers who travelled through. Sadly, there wasn't a shop for the magically inclined, no wands, and certainly none of the rarer spell components a wizard might need. The only things he genuinely wanted could be found near the centre of town at Odds and Ends, a meeting hub and general goods store. Caleb Silvertongue sold everything he needed. Horses and carriages brought supplies in regularly.

After years of adventuring, Yosef trusted his ability to read a crowd. No one appeared to pay him any more attention than usual as he walked to Odds and Ends. The two years he'd spent in Black Hollow meant he was no longer a stranger to the townsfolk. He was liked because of his cakes. A bakery—a rare sight in most towns—was a sweet treat with no equal. In a short amount of time, he had found a place in the town, and, for the most part, while people seemed to like him, they all left him alone. An adventurer with a past he didn't want to talk about. One customer described him as rude, also around the time he hired Nimue to deal with them.

"How can someone so grumpy make such delicious cakes?" he recalled overhearing one day. His family had always known his passion was baker over wizard and, luckily, an irritable temperament worked with both careers.

***

Ayako wasn't used to crowded towns. She grew up with her mother and father in Dragon's Spine, in a small cottage surrounded by rolling hills. Her childhood had been filled with memories of watching the clouds pass by her window, and the sight of the beautiful black dragon with light absorbing scales flying in the sky. But then a living shadow spread across the landscape, and her parents hadn't wanted her to leave the safety of the Spine.

Her desire to see the world hadn't been a passing fancy. There had to be something out there. Her place in the world couldn't be tied to a lone cottage in the middle of nowhere. She'd pestered her parents for months until they'd given in, if only to keep her quiet.

But who'd known the world would be so noisy? She fought the urge to cover her ears, to shield them. Instead, she clutched her hands into fists, determined to prove she could survive outside Dragon's Spine.

After double-checking her hood remained in place, she walked through the busy marketplace. The high collar of her royal-blue cloak hid the scales on the back of her neck, but she still fidgeted. A wide spectrum of races called Black Hollow home, making it clear she wasn't the only person who wasn't human. However, she thought it unlikely any of them hid scales or an impressive heritage tied to dragons.

The townsfolk didn't show kindness to nonhuman races, accepting them grudgingly. And those tainted by dragon blood experienced a difficult life. She was the product of the mating between a black dragon who randomly took human form and a fearless human male. Well, Tomas described himself as fearless. Her mother called him reckless and rather stupid. Ayako didn't think she truly meant the remark since whenever she said it, she often had a smile on her face, hidden behind her strands of black hair.

She had never considered herself to be anything special. Dragons were often targeted by adventurers who wanted their scales for this, that, or the other. Aside from the scales and empathy, the ability to feel and influence other's emotions, she could have been like anyone else.

A small group of women walked past her, carrying baskets and laughing between them. She could almost feel the bonds tying the women together, making them

16

friends.

A life with her family would have been the easiest option. Her mother had hoarded enough gold over the years to last several lifetimes. The treasure promised a simple life, but she wanted more. She craved freedom, a path hers alone. Not one handed to her or expected.

Black Hollow may have been a small town, but the marketplace buzzed with activity. A job should be easy to find. She glanced back at the women, envious.

It took a lot of effort to keep her feet underneath her as she wove through the crowd. The rain from the night before had transformed the ground to slick mud and it was hard to keep her balance. She spied a stall and a man behind the counter, surrounding him were baskets filled with goods and her stomach grumbled at her. There hadn't been time for breakfast as she travelled to Black Hollow through the night. She made her way towards the stall, laughing as she navigated the slippery bog. Suddenly, a sharp jab against her shoulder threw off her precarious balancing act. Ayako spun in the air, arms flailing for balance. Her feet tangled together, and she tumbled to the ground. Thick muck coated the knees of her leggings and the skirt of her dress.

She glanced up sharply, her hand going to her

waist and the dagger she kept there. She didn't have any special abilities tied to her dragon heritage, so Ironchest, the dwarf who lived in a cave in the Dragon's Spine—and had owed her mother a favour— had taught her how to fight, to protect herself. The thing grinning down at her had a mouth filled with broken teeth and two large tusks. Scraggly black hair framed its face—one only a mother could love.

"Hello, little thing, are you lost? My name's Bugrush." The grin grew wider. "What's yours?"

Chapter Two

No one checked to see if she was okay. Ayako suspected nobody would rush to her rescue or her defence. She gritted her teeth and stood.

You can't show fear, lass. That's what they thrive on. Ironchest's words echoed in her head. Pretend you know where you are. Don't ask for advice, and, for the love of the Iron Forged, never go anywhere with a stranger.

She brushed down her dress which did nothing to displace the mud ingrained into the fabric. "I'm not lost." She hoped she sounded more confident than she felt. Life lessons by the dwarf worked well in theory, but she'd never had to put them into practise.

Get into the nearest building. Get yourself surrounded by people or maybe search for the local guard.

She scanned the crowd for someone who might be in charge.

Bugrush placed a rather large hand on her shoulder, and the sheer weight nearly sent her to the ground. She tried to step away, but his grip stopped her. The orc leaned forward, his toxic breath making her eyes water. "I saw you come off the carriage, and you shine so bright. Let me help you. Black Hollow is my town, and I know where everything is."

"No, thank you. My friends are waiting for me." She reached for her dagger in the scabbard at her belt. Her weapon felt pitifully small and unlikely to pierce the orc's skin which resembled the thick flesh on a boar; it might break the blade rather than the flesh. "Let me go."

She frantically glanced around. No one paid them any attention. Would these people seriously let the beast of a man throw her over his shoulder and carry her away? To do with as he pleased. Ayako didn't wait to find out. With a burst of strength, she tugged herself free from his grasp, turned on her heels, and made a run for it.

The busy marketplace she'd been enthralled with earlier meant hiding in a shop wasn't an option. The stalls blocked doors and barrels on the ground and alleyways wouldn't work, either. Unless she wanted to risk jumping over them and ending up in a dead end. *You should always run. You're small and quick. Use the fact to your advantage.* The orc's laughter followed her, and she risked a glance over her shoulder. He resembled a large overenthusiastic puppy, chasing her through the streets.

Then she collided with something hard. The person swore, and she tumbled to the ground, and every muscle screamed in protest. Her whole body burnt with the effort of escape. She tried to get to her feet, but as soon as she put pressure on her foot, it gave way. A yelp escaped her, and, suddenly, there were two hands on the sides of her shoulders, steadying her as she hopped, trying to back away. With her current run of luck, she'd probably landed herself into more trouble.

"You should watch where you're going." The man's voice was brisk and clipped, but when he tried to let her go, she lost her balance again. Ayako glanced up into a pair of dark-brown eyes filled with disdain. His expression softened slightly as her vision blurred with tears. "Are you alright?"

She shook her head.

The man sighed. "This is why I should send Nimue to get ingredients."

"You've caught her, thank you. Hand her over," the orc called out from behind her. "She stole something. I need to retrieve it and take her to the guard."

"He's lying," she cried in protest. "I arrived in town moments ago." There was something about the man in front of her. Anyone else might have been a bit wary about an orc confronting them but not him. A lean build but with an air of power about him. A magic user? The basket on the ground was filled with brown bags. "I'm new to town. All I'm searching for is work. I don't want any trouble."

"A noble task but one you failed at, yes?" The strange man held her gaze for a second. She felt uncomfortable under the intense scrutiny and nearly breathed a sigh of relief when he switched his focus to the orc. "What did the girl steal?"

The orc paused as if scrambling to come up with a believable lie. "Money. My boss's coin purse."

The man smiled coldly. "You're a terrible liar. Do you know who I am?"

He positioned her behind him, her movements far from graceful as she mostly hopped, keeping her full weight off her foot—every time she tried, pain brought fresh tears to her eyes. The man kept his hands free, solidifying her belief he was a magic user. Whenever her mother cast spells, she used a mixture of hand gestures and words.

Bugrush frowned then uncertainty cleared from

his gaze, and his jaw opened slightly before he snapped his mouth shut. The orc's face went wide, an odd look on a face primarily made up of the colour green. "The wizard."

"I see that took a lot of effort. Well done. If you know who I am, you know what I can do. I suggest you apologise to the young lady and get out of my sight before I report you to this town's pathetic excuse for a guard."

"Do you know who I am?" The orc drew himself up to his true height, towering over the wizard.

"You're irrelevant. That's who you are."

A deep rumbling came from Bugrush, but he didn't argue with her rescuer. He turned his attention to her and smiled, and she shuddered. "I'm sure our paths will cross again, bright lady."

Bugrush turned around, knocking over a barrel with his massive frame and sending a pile of fish across the muddy ground. The owner of the stall took one look at the orc and then quietly went to work retrieving and cleaning his goods.

The odd man turned toward her as she hopped in place. "Now, where were we?"

Ayako tried to put weight on her foot, and tears rolled down her cheeks. She shook her head, not trusting her voice.

"I guess you better come with me." He offered his shoulder for her to lean on. He had saved her life, but she didn't even know his name. When she hesitated, he sighed. "My name is Yosef. I own the business Delectable Bites. The bakery. Come with me or don't. It doesn't mean much to me either way."

***

The girl limped after him in silence, her hand on his shoulder to keep her balance. He didn't do random acts of kindness, but he wouldn't have ignored the situation, either, even if she hadn't collided with him with enough speed to nearly take him off his feet. A much larger, brutish man, a full-blood orc, chasing after a human girl for whatever reason was not something, he could pretend he didn't see.

"What are you doing in Black Hollow? Do you have family here?" *Anyone I could drop you off to?*

"No," she whispered, and he glanced at her. The hood on her cloak had fallen, revealing a youthful face and a pained expression. She kept her dark-green hair up in a ponytail, and her dark-blue dress with a high collar ended at the knee. He didn't know much about style, especially on a woman, but it was a very demure appearance. "I'm here to look for work."

"Yes, you did say that."

Her breathing grew laboured, and she swayed on her feet.

Yosef swore and caught her before she collapsed and hit her head. The basket and its contents sprawled onto the ground. Snatching an apple meant for a pie, he threw it at the door to Delectable Bites and yelled for Nimue. A few seconds passed before the door swung open and his assistant peered down at him in sheer bemusement.

"You left to get ingredients. When did they start selling people at Odds and Ends?" She smirked, hands on her hips.

"Maybe instead of laughing, you could help me get her through the door. Then send one of the gnomes to Victor?" The chirurgeon would be much cheaper than getting someone from the temple. The clerics of the Lightbringer cost more than a few coins, and Yosef doubted the girl had the funds to pay for the privilege. Nothing a rest wouldn't cure, but better to be safe than sorry.

Nimue nodded, and she helped him get their guest to her feet who then swayed between them but didn't regain consciousness. "What happened to her?"

"An orc took interest. I didn't recognise him, but

he knew me. At least by reputation. Wait a second. Where do you think you're taking her?" The elf steered the unconscious young lady toward the stairs.

Nimue sighed heavily. "She needs to rest; the best place is a bed. You have any more you're hiding in this place besides yours?"

Damn, he hated when she was right. Not comfortable having a stranger in his bed, he had worked hard on keeping a clear line between him and everyone else. The words he'd spoken to Nimue were the most he had said in weeks. "This is what happens when you aid people. They upend your life," he muttered.

Nimue mumbled something under her breath which sounded a lot like she compared him to an unsociable bear but with more swearing. "You're giving her a place to rest. She'll be awake and gone before you know it." Nimue spent a lot of time with humans, and their mannerisms had rubbed off on her.

They got their charge up the stairs and into his room. He had mostly empty rooms, temporarily holding stock and things he hadn't gotten around to getting rid of in them.

Nimue pushed the sleeping girl into his arms. "Let me make your bed. Do you have clean sheets?"

26

"In the cupboard." He struggled with the girl, the weight of her unnatural to him. When was the last time he'd held someone like this? Had he ever? Carefully, he shuffled her in his arms and lifted her, one arm around her waist and another under her knees. The movement made her head roll back, revealing the smooth column of her neck. Her black eyelashes lay vivid against pale skin.

When Nimue finished, she returned to him, glancing at the female in his arms. "She's rather pretty, don't you think?"

He scowled then positioned her onto his bed.

"Did she happen to mention her name?"

He shook his head. "Doesn't matter. The sooner she wakes up, the sooner she can leave." He tried to keep his voice gruff, not visibly affected by the girl at all.

Nimue burst out laughing, the sound bright and cheerful. "You've always liked a good mystery."

"That's the most ridiculous thing I've ever heard. I don't even know her."

"A girl without a name. Who happens to arrive in town and get attacked within seconds? Surely, it's a puzzle you want to solve?"

"I think you're searching for a mystery where

there isn't any. Get back to work, Nimue. I don't pay you to stand around."

"No, apparently you pay me to help you carry unconscious women to your bed," she replied tartly.

Her tone made what he'd considered a gallant act sound almost sordid. "I couldn't leave her lying in the street."

Chapter Three

When Ayako woke up, there was a mattress beneath her, a light cover over her, and she didn't have a single clue to where she was. She opened her eyes, and panic swirled in the pit of her stomach. She bolted upright, frantically touching her collar, making sure it was still in place. What was the last thing she remembered? Running away from Bugrush and the other man, Yosef? Then limping after him before pain overtook her. The room was dark, fabric across the windows kept the light out. How long had she slept?

"Afternoon." The voice came from nowhere, and she yelped in surprise. She didn't recognize it at all. Distinctly female and full of amusement. "I'm sorry, I didn't mean to startle you, but we thought it would be better if you didn't wake up alone. Don't worry. You're fine. You fainted, and he brought you here."

"Where is here?" She hated how scared she sounded, and she shuffled around until her back pressed against the wall. Promises to her parents about staying safe now seemed empty and hollow.

"This place is called Delectable Bites; it's a bakery.

The Wizard of Black Hollow

My name is Nimue, I work here. What do we call you?"
Suddenly, light exploded into the room as a woman
tugged the curtains apart. Ayako shielded her eyes
before blinking a few times and getting a real look at
the owner of the voice. Vivid green hair and pointy
ears, an odd colour to see on anyone, let alone an elf. A
dress in a matching shade covered curves and dark-
coloured tights covered legs. Still incredibly pretty and
her appearance helped to calm the emotions which
threatened to overwhelm her. The panic slowly ebbed.

Nimue studied her. "You do remember your name,
right? You didn't hit your head when you fell? He said
he caught you."

"It's Ayako."

Nimue smiled. "You're not from around here, are
you?"

"Am I that obvious?" She fought against the urge
to touch the back of her neck. The collar hadn't been
disturbed which meant they hadn't seen the scales.
Touching it would only bring attention to it, so she
clasped her hands together stopping herself. "What
gave me away?"

Nimue tipped her head to the side, crossed her
arms, and studied her. She didn't have much
experience with elves, but the playful look in the

woman's gaze vanished and was replaced by something far older. Elves aged at a slower rate than humans and there was no telling how old the elf was. The way she studied her made Nimue appear older, the happy and careful persona shifting to that of a teacher.

"You're dressed like a traveller. The bag you brought with you has clothes in it and a small pouch of gold. An educated guess." A large smile broke out across her face, and the old learnt expression disappeared completely.

"Good guess." The elf's ability to read her so thoroughly was a little disconcerting. She glanced down at her covered feet. "Where are my boots?"

"He told me you hurt your ankle. Couldn't really leave the boots on as it was starting to swell. I assumed you'd rather have them removed than cut off of you." Nimue walked towards her and sat on the bed. Carefully, she pulled the cover up and revealed her ankle. An ugly black bruise greeted her. As the cover was moved, dragging across her skin, she bit back a scream of pain.

She sighed. "My first war wound. I really thought it would take me longer to get one." She reached down and prodded the skin. The brief contact sent a fresh wave of pain over her. "Do you think you can help me get to the nearest inn?" She needed to find somewhere to stay until she recovered. There was enough gold in the pouch to pay for a few days.

Nimue waved in the air. "He spent the last few hours sorting out one of the rooms. You can stay here. I don't want to hear any protests."

"He's already helped me enough as it is," she protested anyway.

The elven woman smiled at her brightly. "Yosef isn't known for his desire to help others. At least, not anymore. It surprised me as well. He's a good man, and you'll be safe here. I promise. He is a little abrupt and has no real like for anyone. Still a good place as any to rest up until you're back on your feet."

"Surely, there's a temple or a cleric who can heal it?"

"Black Hollow isn't a big town, so they charge a lot of money for their services. It's a bruised foot, Ayako. A few days and you'll be back on your way." Nimue got off the bed and straightened her skirt. "He did get you something he thought might help." She walked to the door, retrieved two long sticks with triangles on the top of them, and handed them to her. After a quick set of instructions on how to use them, she risked getting to her feet. A few wobbly moments later, she was able to move without falling over. "Let's head downstairs, and I'll introduce you to the gentlemen."

She had hoped she would have more time to practise in the privacy of the room, but there was an air about Nimue which made it obvious she wouldn't take no for an answer.

It took longer than it should have to get down the stairs. She fought to keep her balance on her remaining good foot. A trip which should have taken seconds took a few minutes. Nimue carried one of the sticks, and Ayako used the other, her free hand on the handrail. When they eventually reached the bottom, Nimue returned the stick. There was a smell of baked goods in the air, but the hour must have been early since the store was empty. A steady chatter of noise came from beyond the counter and an open door. Nimue helped her past the counter and into the room, which turned out to be a kitchen. Two gnomes glanced up from their workstations. One had a head full of blond hair, a thick short beard, and an apron over simple clothes. The other had dark hair, almost black, and a clean-shaven face. He also wore an apron and his clothes like his working companion.

"This is Tamlic and Catlo. Otherwise known as the

Gentlemen, this is Ayako. She'll be staying with us until she is back on her feet."

The one whom she called Tamlic peered at Ayako, curious. "Is she the reason he's been in a worse mood than usual?"

Catlo burst into laughter. "How could you tell; his mood is always the same."

She glanced at Nimue, panicked. "I did say I could stay in the inn. I don't want to inconvenience anyone." She guessed she wasn't a welcomed guest after all.

Nimue waved a hand at her, but it did little to dismiss her fears. "Don't be silly. He said you could stay. He wants to help."

Tamlic snorted. "He hasn't helped anyone for a long time. What changed?"

A door leading outside opened, and the man in question swept into the kitchen. Swept—sounded so dramatic but was the best word to describe him. A wizard. It explained his regal carriage, the way he held his head high. Ayako wasn't sure she liked the man who'd saved her life. He cast a cursory glance around the room, his gaze lingering on her for a split second. She smiled, and his expression softened slightly before hardening again, and he turned his attention to the gnome.

"Your pay did, Tamlic, for the worse. It'll go up again when you show some respect. How are you feeling?" The latter comment had been directed at her.

"I-I'm good, thank you," she stuttered.

He reminded her of Ironchest, the dwarf who lived in a cave near her parents' home. A brisk, cold man who became her teacher of sorts. He hadn't been a wizard, but both men appeared to be cut from the same cloth. They spoke and expected to be listened to.

"A few days of rest, and her foot will be as good as new. I don't think it's broken." From her place at the table, Nimue picked up one of the small cakes, a small thing with pink frosting on the top, and took a bite.

He cocked an eyebrow, and, for a second, looked like he might comment. But he didn't. His personality was a little abrupt, but the gnomes and elf didn't seem too upset or thrown by it. Odd combination. There had to be something they liked about him for them to continue to work with him. Also, they trusted she was safe with him. Ayako planned to spend the time in her makeshift room. She couldn't believe she was staying with a man she didn't know. If Beltrix could see her now, she would be horrified and would probably try and eat him. A sheltered upbringing and now she was going to share a home with a man she didn't even know, for a few days. Her father would be worried but probably a little impressed.

"Well, I've sorted out a temporary room. Keep to yourself and we'll be fine." Yosef swept out of the room.

She frowned, and Tamlic laughed softly.

"He isn't much of a knight in shining armour, lass."

"I don't understand why he wants me to stay when it's obvious he doesn't want me here." She managed to position herself by the counter.

Nimue pushed a cake towards her. She'd never seen anything like it. Small enough to fit into the palm of her hand with a thick cream-like substance on the top. Ayako gingerly reached out, scooping a little of the strange gloop up with her fingertip. The others watched her closely as she brought it to her lips. As soon as it touched her tongue, sensations swept over her. Sweetness like she'd never experienced sent a jolt of energy through her, she widened her eyes in surprise.

"What is this?" she managed to say as she took another bite.

"He calls them cupcakes." Nimue smiled brightly at her. "He's a complicated man, but I have to believe a cruel person couldn't create things like this. I think helping you is going to help him more."

She nodded—she slept with a blade underneath her pillow anyway. A little naive maybe, but she wasn't an idiot—then bit into the cupcake again, stopping herself short of moaning in delight.

Chapter Four

He kept himself busy, reducing the chances of bumping into his guest. Nimue delivered food to her, and Yosef knew she practised using her crutches travelling up and down the hallway, by the steady thumps he heard from the floor above. Boredom must have been settling in because she ventured a little further each day. He heard Catlo ask if she wanted to help in the kitchen, but she didn't know how to bake. Their paths rarely crossed because the odd girl didn't spend too much time on the ground floor. And he was more than happy about the distance between them.

Yosef arrived at Odds and Ends early, the shop doors in the process of being unlocked. Caleb Silvertongue, an elf with long white hair and a keen sense for business, glanced at him in surprise but didn't comment. As he went out the back to collect the ingredients Yosef needed, he found himself searching the shelves. Sometimes, a cursory glance revealed an interesting tidbit he could use in a new recipe. Experimenting always filled him with a sense of accomplishment, especially when the results turned out well. As he searched, his gaze fell on a book. He picked it up, confused. *Beasts and Unseen Monsters in the Madore Kingdom*? Strange thing to find in the general store.

"If you want it, it's two gold," Caleb called from his place behind the counter.

"You don't sell books. Where did this come from?"

The elf shrugged. "Someone left it here. Nobody has returned for it, so now I can sell it." His long white hair was tied back with a simple band and his pointy ears proudly on display. Black Hollow wasn't fond of those who were different but did like those who paid their way. Caleb brought business to the town and sold things people needed. Anything considered hard to find or next to impossible to locate, Caleb found a way. Nobody could fault his work ethic or skill. Like most people of his kind, he was tall and slender. Graceful. Words often used to describe himself, but the elves put him to shame.

"You're all heart, Silvertongue."

He wrote something down on a sheet of parchment with a quill. "Shouldn't have left it here. Do you want it or not?"

He closed the book. He didn't have any use for it, but it would give the girl something to do. "One gold."

He put it in his basket ready to join the other small bags. "I buy a lot from you. It's more than fair. Especially since the book didn't belong to you to begin with." He approached the counter and put the basket on top ready for Caleb to put his purchases in. In the event Ayako couldn't read, the pictures might entertain her.

"A gold and a silver."

Yosef cocked an eyebrow and sighed. "It is too early in the day to barter with any real skill. How about a gold and a copper?" He picked up the book. "Or I could leave it here? It doesn't matter to me either way."

Caleb reluctantly agreed to the deal, and he paid for his goods before picking his basket and leaving. The sun crested over the mountain range, casting everything in a warm glow. There was a gentle hum of activity in the shop as he entered through the back door. A mug of hot coffee waited for him, a marvellous invention, a little bitter but it would chase away the last dregs of sleep which clung to him. He gave a silent nod of thanks to no one before leaving the basket, retrieving the book, and went to head upstairs.

The gnomes didn't pay him any attention; he assumed Nimue made the drink since they only spoke to him when Nimue wasn't around. The humming from the counter a reminder she was already hard at work. The book would probably be the subject of conversation later.

With the book wedged underneath his arm, he held his cup, and with his free hand made sure he didn't trip over his robe as he travelled upstairs. He stopped in front of her door for a second, unsure about what to do next. Should he knock on the door and hand the book to her or leave it outside? He stood there for a moment, torn. They hadn't exchanged more than a handful of words. Busy, that was what he had been. Too busy to see if the girl he had rescued, and possibly kidnapped, was okay. He hadn't thought about the implications. Instead, he'd focused on the fact she was a stranger in the town, attacked and needing assistance. He'd offered her a place to stay, even if he hadn't wanted to. Nimue was the one who'd insisted she stayed. Pointless to argue with the elf, no good ever came of it. He closed his eyes and rubbed the bridge of his nose. Solid reasoning for not having friends. Conversations were awkward. Friendships even more so.

The door opened.

She gasped in obvious surprise, and Yosef opened

his eyes, instinctively stepping away. Nimue had given her a few dresses to wear but she wore ones she brought with her; this one also had a high neck, the fabric a dull shade of blue. He suspected it had to be one of her own—a little too prim and proper for the elf.

Maybe she came from money, explaining her fondness for formal dresses. Either way, the dress suited her. Her black hair, which had a slight curl to it, was down, heavy and thick across her shoulders.

"Yosef." She glanced up at him with mesmerizing green eyes. Beautiful.

He shook his head, hoping the movement would dislodge the random thought.

"Why are you here? I mean, of course, you can be here. This is your home." A lovely pink glow enveloped her face. "I mean, good morning, Yosef."

He handed her the book, and her gaze widened slightly.

"You brought me something?"

He nodded. The girl threw him completely off-balance, making him proverbially tongue-tied. Yosef could be accused of many things but being at a lack of words had never been one of them. "I thought you might like something to read as you rested. How is your foot?"

She glanced down, and he followed her gaze. Her feet were naked, and she wriggled her toes. There was still a purple sheen around her ankle but not as bad as it first appeared. "It still hurts a little." She glanced at the book in her hands. "Thank you for this. I like reading."

"Would you like something else to do? I mean, if you're bored."

Ayako held the book to her chest and nodded, the movement setting her heavy hair over her shoulders, reframing her face.

"Nimue has been asking me for some time to visit family who live near The Silver Tree. An elven city to the west. I'm not one for customers; it's not in my skill set. You could help." He had no clue what he was doing. Nimue had asked for time off, but that had been months ago. A request he denied. She'd be thrilled at the idea. "Do you think you could do that?"

"I could give it a try." She smiled, shyly. "Thank you, I was starting to climb the walls."

"You do know you're more than welcome to come downstairs, sit at one of the tables." Why was he offering this to her? He'd been doing his best, ensuring their paths didn't cross, and now he was inviting her downstairs? He fought against the urge to rub his

44

forehead. "Working the counter means you don't have to move around very much. I could find you a stool."

"That is really sweet of you." She appeared confused. He guessed he hadn't shown her many sides of his personality besides his standard grumpy one. "If it's no trouble."

"Not at all."

The frown gave way to a beautiful smile, which made her eyes shine. "I'll head downstairs and talk to Nimue. I should probably ask what her job actually entails."

She made to move out of her room, but he raised his hand, stopping her mid-step. "I'll send her up to you." He gestured to her feet. "You're not wearing any shoes."

Ayako blushed, an enchanting sight to be sure. "I can put some on. They're a little tight at the moment but they fit, for the most part. If I don't lace them."

"I insist." He needed to talk to Nimue first so she would be less surprised to learn he'd changed his mind. "Anyway, it'll be the perfect time to read the book."

"Good idea. Thank you for this." She raised the book before shutting the door.

He closed his eyes and rested his head against the

solid frame. After taking a few cleansing breaths, he went in search of Nimue.

Chapter Five

There had been many things she could have seen when she opened the door. She never would have expected him. There was no way she could mask her surprise at seeing him, standing in the doorway with a book in his hand, his eyes closed as if trapped in his own thoughts, working up the courage to knock on her door?

He was hard to read, even with her empathy. She didn't think she affected him at all. She could count on one hand how many times they'd spoken over the last few days. If anything, it felt like he was avoiding her.

Ayako climbed back onto her bed, crossed her legs underneath the skirt of her borrowed dress, and flipped open the book, skimming the pages. She'd grown up with books on a range of different subjects. With an overprotective mother who hoarded books, and a dwarf tutor who liked to use them to teach. She preferred storybooks, but there was something intensely comforting about holding one in her hand. With no siblings and not being able to travel out of the Spine, they were her means of escape, to visit other countries, thanks to the words on the page.

Ironchest had also collected them over the course of his adventuring life, a habit he shared with Beltrix the Black, a hoarder of precious things. Her mother preferred gold coins, but books were held in high regard. She still struggled to figure out what gave her own life meaning. Quests like the ones the adventurer had in the books she liked to read? Those stories inspired her to be fearless and brave. Even if she never felt like that.

A laugh escaped her as Ironchest's words ringed in her ears. You can't trust the tales of adventurers. They won't tell you the bad, the moments they cracked under pressure. No adventure, quest or otherwise, is without hardship and loss. Another pearl of wisdom. Although, his words hadn't done much to squish her desires to have an adventure of her own.

A brisk knock on the door was her only warning as Nimue strolled in, a scowl on her face. Her vibrant-green hair was clipped up, with strands braided in an intricate style. A navy-blue corset pulled in her white tunic at the waist, and her skirt ended a little below the knee. She resembled a barmaid, a striking choice of clothing for an elf.

"Nimue, what's wrong?"

The annoyance vanished, as if it hadn't been there to begin with. She smiled brightly, but there was something false about her demeanour, as if she was hiding something. She frowned, trying to pinpoint what the problem was. Empathy wasn't a useful skill. The rare flashes of emotions were difficult to read at the best of times, so she'd never put much faith in what she felt from others. "It's nothing. Yosef had a chat with me. Looks like I'm going on a trip."

She patted the bed, inviting her friend to sit. "I thought you wanted to see your family?"

Nimue sat down opposite her, crossing her legs and lying on the bed. "I do." She waved at the air, as if she was fighting off imagery bugs. "I'm a little surprised. All I asked for was a few days, but he ignored my request. Yosef's problem is simple. He doesn't know how to handle customers, and he doesn't trust the gnomes. I doubt he'll ever leave them in charge. Delectable Bites is popular as well. A blessing and a curse."

"Which one am I? The blessing or the curse?"

The elf laughed. "Definitely a blessing. If you don't take my job from me, we'll be fine. He would be the curse." The smile faded.

"You must like him at least a little, or why else

49

would you work for him?" She closed the book, more than a little interested in finding out more about the wizard.

Nimue rolled onto her side, her hand underneath her head, studying her. "Yosef is a complicated man, as I've mentioned before. Two years ago, he came to this town a broken man. Everyone could see it. Doesn't matter how hard someone holds themselves. How they talk to others or don't in his case. It's in the eyes. You can tell who's been damaged by the things they've seen."

"What did he see?"

She sat up, moving until her back was against the wall. "Let me tell you what you're expected to do while I'm gone. It'll be for a week, barely any time." It didn't escape her notice Nimue hadn't answered her question at all.

When Nimue told her another story of a customer who declared his love for her, to beg her to run away with him, Ayako had a hard time not laughing. The elf had a natural charm, one she couldn't hope to emulate. It didn't surprise her in the slightest men fell in love with her. The customers were going to be disappointed when they found out she was replacing her. "I have no intention of stealing hearts while I'm here. I promise."

"There are plenty of women here as well. Some of them might like their hearts stolen." The elf spoke so casually, for a second, Ayako must have misheard.

Her face heated. "I've never had much time or opportunity to think about either," she replied honestly. Interactions with anyone who wasn't family, or a grumpy dwarf, had been practically impossible when she was growing up. She glanced at the book. An unexpected gift. The only time her curiosity had been piqued was with the wizard. Strange. She hadn't had much interaction with him, and when she had, she'd ended up confused.

Understanding dawned in the elf's eyes. "You've never been with anyone, have you?"

Her face burnt hotter. "I've lived a sheltered life. Fairly sure my mother would have bitten the head off any boy, girl, or otherwise if they'd looked at me the wrong way." The words left her in a wild rush.

"Don't worry, Ayako, I'm teasing you. Promise not to steal my job?"

"It's safe with me," she promised. Thankfully, Nimue didn't ask more questions about her family, a subject she would gladly never elaborate on. If she did, it would be lies, and she didn't want to lie to Nimue.

"Speaking of jobs. Who's doing yours while you're up here with me?"

"Tamlic. And since there haven't been any loud explosions while I've been up here, I'm sure everything's fine. The gnomes are good people. You'll be safe with them."

"And Yosef, what can you tell me about him?" She aimed for nonchalant. Nimue had deflected the question earlier, but she wanted to know more. The wizard was a puzzle missing half of the pieces. A talented magic caster with a reputation that made an orc run without even casting a spell. How had a man like him end up running a bakery of all things?

A small smile curled Nimue's lip. "He's an enigma and he doesn't like talking about his past. You must promise you won't tell him I told you. I need your word."

"You have it."

She studied her expression, and Ayako couldn't help but wonder if she could read the truth in her words. After a moment, the other woman nodded, apparently happy with whatever she saw. "He used to be an adventurer. A member of a group known as the Mockery. Have you heard of them?"

She shook her head. "Strange name for a group."

She didn't have much in the way of experiences with adventuring parties besides the accounts she read. Her mother was a different story though. Even though she never mentioned her past life—because who would tell tales of murder and chaos to a small child? —her mother had killed more than her fair share of adventurers. Those who wanted her hoard of treasure or body parts. Scales for potions. Eyes for scrying spells. Blood for poisons. The thought made her shudder in disgust. Every being had the right to live if they didn't hurt others, and Beltrix the Black only killed in self-defence.

"They were an odd group of people. Gnomes. Dwarves and halflings. I believe there were also goblins thrown into the mix. A mockery of a real group," Nimue explained, oblivious to Ayako's sudden discomfort. "One day, a job went wrong. He was the only one who walked away. I believe he still has nightmares, though he's never talked about them."

Ayako inched closer. "What happened?"

"They were killed by the dragon they hunted." Nimue whispered the words, and Ayako glanced at the door, suddenly worried he would barge in and overhear them talking.

The blood drained from her face. "What colour

was the dragon?"

"Does it matter?" Nimue shrugged. "Gold, I think."

She fought against the urge to breathe a sigh of relief. Gold was incredibly rare—the only one being the Golden Dawn. There was no real sense of community between the dragons. It wasn't like they met up for meals and chatted about things. If anything, they fought tooth and claw over territory. It was ridiculous. If they banded together, they could help keep their kind from extinction. There were so few of them. "That's horrible. Why did they go after the dragon? I mean, it's pretty much a death sentence for anyone." Adventurers could kill one of them, but the group usually had years of experience and luck on their side. A lot of luck.

"Black Hollow was in the midst of a horrible disease—"

"They were told the scales would help with a cure," she said, not needing Nimue to finish the sentence. A key component for healing potions. Not all kinds but the most potent ones. She absentmindedly touched her own scales, still hidden underneath the collar of the dress. She would be an easy target for anyone who knew and desired them. They would fetch a lot of coin to the right buyer. Having them pried out of her skin with a knife? She shuddered at the thought.

"He managed to get away, and the scales did help. But there wasn't enough to cure the entire town. He tried to talk the officials into giving the cure to the children and the elderly." A pained expression returned to Nimue's eyes.

"But they didn't?"

She shook her head. "The cure was given to the officials. A lot of people died, because of their poor decision, he changed a little more, his view of the world twisting, leaving him with an intense dislike for authority and things with scales."

Chapter Six

Yosef kept the office door closed. An open one encouraged idle chitchat, not from the people who worked for him, they knew better, but others... As soon as he accidently made eye contact with a customer, they became emboldened and asked questions. What was the point of having a reputation if he didn't lean into it sometimes? Grumpy. Unapproachable. Words which described him perfectly and he embraced.

With the paperwork laid out in front of him, he wrote up the daily and weekly shopping lists. When he was finished, he glanced at the weekly intakes, taking note of what was selling and what wasn't then amended the list of things he needed to purchase. Usually, nothing broke through his intense focus. Paperwork wasn't interesting, but it helped to shake the nightmares following him throughout the day and pulled him into a world all his own.

Today, however, had been different. Her laughter broke his focus several times He'd had to make a few hours of mumbled apologies, but the girl was coming out of her shell.

The Wizard of Black Hollow

The customers were full of questions. Where was Nimue? Was she okay? When would she be back? He found himself listening in on the conversations. Would Ayako let slip more about her past? She played her cards close to her chest—a skill he admired. Approachable but intensely private. Different from Nimue, whose voice grated on him. Ayako's was almost musical, and he absentmindedly wondered if she sang.

The thoughts irked him. He'd only known her for a short amount of time. How was he becoming attached to her? A path which only led to heartbreak and pain. Everyone had secrets. She was no different. Nobody showed their true face. He learnt that lesson the hard way with Wizard Branch, a person he'd trusted and who'd effectively sent him and his party to their deaths. No, he would be much safer to keep his distance. A few more days and Nimue would return and his life would be normal again.

"Yosef?"

He glanced up, surprised. Ayako stood in the doorway, one of the crutches underneath her arm. In her free hand, she carried an envelope. "What is it?"

"This was delivered for you." She hobbled across to him and passed the missive over. He noticed the tremble in her hand. Possibly nerves or the stress of having to move around with the crutch? Did he make her nervous? If it eased her thoughts at all, she inspired the feeling in him as well. The envelope weighed heavily against his palm. "I didn't see who dropped it off. I turned around for a second, and it appeared on the counter."

The news made his heart sink a little, and he raised the pristine envelope to his nose, breathing in deeply. Magic left a trace. A recognisable smell, like brimstone and sandalwood. "Don't worry about it. I have a good feeling I know the person who sent this." He put the missive on his desk, not bothering to check the contents. There were always complications when someone tried to do the right thing. Either the gesture was accepted or refused—even if he'd meant the best intentions.

"Do you want to talk about it?" Ayako asked as she stepped into the office and closed the door behind her. "We're not busy, and Nimue said I could take a break around this time. The gnomes are in the middle of making batches for tomorrow. I even remembered to lock the front door and put the sign in the window." She hobbled over to the chair opposite him and sat down...without asking for his permission.

"You seem to be doing well out there."

"I am," she replied with a small smile. "Now, don't change the subject."

He frowned, a little unsure about what to do. She'd offered to listen, but it had been a long time since he'd talked to anyone. He shook his head. "No, I don't want to talk about it." He glanced down at his order slips, essentially dismissing her. She stayed in her seat. "You can go." She didn't move. This time he glared at her with his trademark scowl. "I said you can leave. Are you hard of hearing?"

She barely batted an eyelash, instead shaking her head. "I'm entitled to a break. It doesn't say where I need to take it." She laid the crutch next to her chair, and clasped her hands primly in her lap.

The girl confused the hell out of him. There was no point in denying it. Others would have left. Hadn't he put enough loathing into his voice? He rubbed the palm of his hand against his forehead. "You really aren't going to leave?"

This was his own fault, letting Nimue talk him into letting her stay while she recuperated. A stranger in a new city. His good deed wasn't going to go unpunished. The girl from a few days ago would have left him to his thoughts, but she'd become comfortable in his presence.

She smiled brightly at him. There was still something guarded behind her expression. She might have wanted him to share his secrets, but he doubted she would be so forthcoming with her own. "I'm not going anywhere. I might not have much experience with people. My upbringing was sheltered at the best of times, but even I know you shouldn't wallow in self-pity or pain. Not if someone is willing to listen."

He scowled. "I don't need anyone."

"I'm going to leave in a few days. Either I'll find work in the town or go back home. We'll probably never see each other again. If you can't talk to someone who you will never see again, who can you talk to?" His heart twisted uncomfortably at her words. She leaned forward, her dark braid draping over her shoulder. There they were again. The green eyes that held him in his place, encouraged him to share his secrets. "Tell me what's bothering you."

A part of him wanted to hold fast to his resolve. In the name of all the gods, who did this girl think she was? Demanding he open a part of himself he kept hidden for a reason, like she had a right to see it. To bear witness to his pain. A tiny voice in the back of his skull told him she was right. He wouldn't be asking her to stay after she was well. Nothing held her here. What harm would come from giving voice to the things plaguing him?

Weakness.

The word hit him hard; he didn't want to show weakness. He closed his eyes, reached out, and touched the envelope with the tips of his fingers. "I don't know what Nimue told you. There's no point in denying it. Nimue is a force of nature and rarely holds fast to rules. Especially ones given by me. Odd for an elf, but she wouldn't have left without telling you about my past. The dragon." The mere mention of the word recalled the golden beast, the screams of pains, the deafening sound of its roar. "Five people died. We weren't friends, more like colleagues thrown together by strange circumstances. Like the gods had played a hand in our meeting. Gru, Grogswald, Dust, Sticky, and Polgrund. Members left and came back. Grogswald left early on after he found his granddaughter who, when our paths crossed again, made me promise I would keep an eye on him. He was an old goblin, didn't have a knack for names." Without much thought, he put both hands on either side of the envelope. He could still picture Elsbeth's face. Pretty for a goblin. Green skin, large tusks, and long pointed ears. She had lost all her family and hadn't been best pleased when Grogswald offered to help against the dragon.

"What happened to him?"

The screams hit him like the years hadn't passed. Like he was still in the cave. The rhythmic sound of raindrops on stone. The chill in the air. "Sticky died first. Next Polgrund. He ran at the beast, screaming, with his sword held high. A complete and utter idiot. I tried to stop him. I knew how foolish the whole situation was. What kind of person went up against a dragon? One who wanted to end up in an early grave. Then Dust and Gru, who made a habit of pissing off deities." He raised his hand, stopping her from pursuing the train of thought. "It's long and complicated. A story for a different time. But he must have prayed to the correct one because he was able to retrieve the scales which had fallen out of Polgrund's hand and landed on the ground. The dragon lashed out with his claws, raking into his back, taking him to his knees." He touched the sides of his head as tears sprang to his eyes. "He threw the bag at me, but it was Grogswald who grabbed them. Me and Grogswald stood side by side, throwing spells at this thing, but nothing stuck. It was old, powerful. We were going to die. I knew it with every ounce of my being. Grogswald knew it, too. He sacrificed himself to get me out, far enough away that my teleportation spell wouldn't be countered. Old fool. I didn't like any of them. They knew that." He couldn't keep the pain out of his voice as he thought about them.

There was a long pause. "Yosef."

He glared at her. "Is this what you wanted to hear, how a bunch of monsters gave up their lives to save mine? How poorly I treated them?" There was so much pity in her eyes, he could barely stand it. He needed to be alone. Sharing his thoughts with her had been a terrible idea. "Get out."

She slowly bent down, retrieved her crutch, and walked to the office door. "The envelope is from Elsbeth, isn't it?"

"I don't want to talk about it anymore, Ayako. Please leave me alone."

For a brief second, she might have obeyed his request, but she hadn't before, so why would she now? "You constantly say you didn't like them. I get the impression you don't like many people, but I also think you've become particularly good at lying to yourself."

"And pray tell, how do you come to such a conclusion?" he replied, his tone harsh.

"Because you're crying, Yosef." She opened the

door. "Someone who doesn't care wouldn't cry over the death of a few monsters."

Chapter Seven

She yawned as she collapsed onto the bed and closed her eyes. Yosef had remained hidden for the remainder of the day. The message couldn't have been clearer. She'd pushed him too hard and now he didn't want to talk to her at all. She couldn't blame him for the decision. The pain had rolled off him in almost tangible waves. Being truthful was supposed to be cathartic, and he'd kept himself bottled up for far too long. The letter helped but as soon as he revealed the thoughts he kept hidden, he shut down completely.

A part of her should have hated him. He hunted a dragon. One who hadn't asked for the attack and defended herself. The fact his friends died meant he'd learnt his lesson, a harsh but necessary one. Would he have hunted her if he knew the truth? She didn't have any abilities tied to her dragon heritage, and she doubted her scales could be used for a cure to anything. But a desperate man who wanted to heal a village or town wouldn't listen to reason. Her empathy helped, telling her he was a good man, which was the only reason she hadn't run out of the door.

She rolled onto her side and touched her scales. They were smooth under her fingertips and brought her some relief, calming her thoughts. She didn't know what to do. Write her parents a letter, asking for advice? It would take weeks to get there, and there was no guarantee a messenger would risk travelling into the Spine. Beltrix wasn't the best person to ask. Very much in the burn and kill them all, she wouldn't encourage her only daughter to go on a killing spree though. Her father, on the other hand, was much more even tempered. She sighed. Two weeks was too long a wait to ask. The round trip would take a month. Ayako didn't even know what she would be doing by the end of the week.

Maybe the talking helped? Maybe it would be enough for Yosef to get over the pain holding him back?

Screams had erupted in the middle of the night more than once. A sudden yelp...as if nightmares had awakened him. Could a talk be enough to stop them?

No. He was stubborn. He would hold onto his grief until the day he died. There wasn't much she could do if he didn't want help.

She rolled onto her side and picked up the book he gave her. After hitching herself up until she rested against the pillow, she ran her hand over the cover of the book. Yosef wasn't lost. She had to believe that. He needed to accept the fact he lost friends, that he viewed them as more than monsters. He fought the knowledge and, maybe by doing so, stopped himself from grieving and moving on. He was filled with prejudgments against those who were different, but she doubted he felt the same now. He couldn't.

Tamlic and Catlo made her a simple meal of bread and meat cutlets. The bakery supplied the bread, but she was sure one of them had travelled to the local inn for the meats. They really were quite sweet. Light and shadow. The perfect pair making a whole. Both thought they needed to show her kindness because Yosef appeared incapable. The book was proof he had a kind heart. Both of them and Nimue stayed for a reason. It couldn't be because work was hard to find.

She wouldn't get answers from the book in front of her, but she started to read anyway. The wizard was a problem for another day.

Hours passed before he left his office again, the paperwork completed, the shopping lists for the month done. In the end, he picked a book from the shelf and read until the bakery went quiet, the gnomes yelling goodbye to Ayako as they left. After the distinct sounds of her sliding a bolt to lock the door, her footsteps on the stairs, he collected the money for the day then spent another hour counting the gold, silver, and copper pieces. This part certainly wasn't the reason he wanted to be a baker, though the simple act was oddly soothing.

He glanced at the stairs before he walked into the kitchen, running his hands over the clean counters and the jarred ingredients. Quite a while had passed since he'd been able to get into the kitchen and bake anything himself. He needed to find some time, when the bakery was closed, and his inner sanctum was quiet. He put out recipe slips onto the counter for the gnomes in the morning before returning to the safety of the office. He'd always preferred the rich aromas over the smell of musty scrolls. There was a feeling of accomplishment when something came out of the hot oven perfectly risen. A little like a spell. In the end, however, he hadn't even become a baker, not really. Instead, he had become a banker.

The thought made him shudder and almost wish to become an adventurer again. Almost.

Finished, he put the money into the safe with the ledger which held an incredibly detailed description of the businesses they dealt with. Yosef slowly walked up to his room, deliberately avoiding looking at her door. Treating it like a dangerous beast that would attack if he got too close.

He considered himself a closed book. Not easy to read at all. Somehow, the girl had managed to get him to open himself up, to admit things he'd kept hidden. Something which should have been impossible. Yosef wasn't swayed by a pretty face.

So...she wasn't completely human. But what? Spellcasting left a trace, one easy to read, and he hadn't detected anything.

He walked away from the door, pointedly ignoring the urge to knock. He still didn't trust her or anyone.

He went into his room, immediately noticing the plate of food left in front of the door. There wasn't a note, but it had to have been Ayako. Picking up the plate heavy with a small bread roll, meats, and a cake piled on top, he took the food into his room, putting the dish on a table near the bed. He sat down, kicked off his boots, and picked up the bread.

There were plenty of spells used to compel someone to tell the truth. Some involved hand gestures or particular words to trigger them. She hadn't done either. He bit into the bread then went to his bookcase.

71

The Wizard of Black Hollow

Books were expensive but invaluable. He collected them on quests. It was always a surprise to see what a person left in a chest.

He dragged his fingers across the spines. Races indigenous to the area. Spells. History. He flipped the first book open, a heavy tomb made from leather, a gift from an old mentor. The pages had yellowed, crisp underneath his hands, so he needed to be careful. The pictures were hand drawn, a few painted, and was a prized possession and quite beautiful, even if the images they depicted weren't. Monsters. Trolls. Dragons. Something only to be found in the sea, the name for the beast unclear since the handwriting was smeared and dulled. Braxton died months ago, and the book had been delivered to him with things Braxton thought he might like. Parting gifts. The man told him he had talent. The potential to be a great wizard, even if he didn't want to be one.

"You can't deny the power inside of you. To deny it is to taunt it. The power doesn't go away because you don't want it but pushes beneath your skin, wanting to be used."

The notes next to the image said whatever the creature was, it preferred water and didn't have the ability of empathy which he believed Ayako possessed.

He couldn't tell if she had ill intent. How bad was it to confront the pain of a person's past? Was it healthier to confront it or bury it deep?

Yosef closed the book with an audible thump. She wasn't a monster, but she was certainly something. He, on the other hand, could be described as many things and maybe even a monster. But he wasn't an idiot.

He'd failed them. They all died that day, and, only because of them, he was alive. When had the monsters in his party become his friends? The first day he met them had been at the Baron's Keep. The Baron's right-hand man, McLellan, had put the party together. Hired to fight the monsters plaguing the area, and the only human in a party full of races the surrounding areas barely tolerated, he'd assigned himself as their keeper. He wouldn't have cared if they had died. If anything, their deaths would have made his life simpler. He would have been placed with the other adventurers. The ones without scales or a taste for raw flesh.

But being with them taught him a lot—even though he'd been loathed to admit the truth at the time. They were very much like the humans in the Madore Kingdom. They made poor decisions. They joked and laughed. They also had horrible taste in food. Yosef shuddered at the memory of Grogswald's "soup." All of them had a beating heart, even if their blood was a different colour from his. They kept each other safe like a dysfunctional family. Even if he hadn't made his dislike of them a secret. They hadn't treated him any differently.

Because, in a group of monsters, he'd been the odd one out, and they hadn't judged him for it.

He put the book back onto the shelf. Whatever Ayako was, she kept it secret for a reason. She hadn't hurt anyone, and all she'd tried to do was help. It was possible she didn't even know what she was or what she could do.

Could be something incredibly simple. And perhaps he wasn't as immune to a pretty face as he first thought? When was the last time Yosef had a relationship with anyone but himself? He shrugged off his robes and got himself into clothes to sleep in. Damn, he couldn't remember. Who had time for a relationship when a man was busy berating himself for the decisions he made? He glanced at the door, which opened into the hallway. He crossed his arms then rubbed his bottom lip with his thumb, deep in thought. What could it be?

A simple but dangerous magic, but when he lingered on it, the truth of his thought hit him with a clarity he hadn't thought possible, and everything snapped into sharp focus.

"Dammit." He stalked across the room and closed the door with a little more force than necessary. A few more days and she'd be gone. A few more days. How bad could that be?

Chapter Eight

Yosef walked down the stairs and disappeared into the kitchen without even sparing her a glance. His annoyance, almost a tangible thing, shielded him. Ayako couldn't believe encouraging him to open up had been such a bad thing. She closed her eyes and rested her hands on the counter, breathed in deeply, and let out a sigh. Possibly, he viewed her as a nuisance and nothing more, and if that were the case, what was the point in trying to help him? He didn't want her to.

Every time the door opened, she glanced over, half hoping he would appear. By the afternoon, it was obvious he wasn't coming back anytime soon. Both Tamlic and Catlo had popped their heads out to ask if she had seen him. Apparently, for him to be out for the entire day was rare.

None of the customers asked about him though. Not like they'd enquired about Nimue. Did he prefer things that way? He supplied the baked goods. The customers brought the coin. But if the cakes stopped completely...well, then there would be a problem.

Sugar was addictive. The whole town might end up rioting. She grinned at the impossible thought. *How silly is that?* Nimue would be home in two days, and she had promised the elf the building would still be standing when she came back.

She gingerly put weight on her ankle, but, besides the odd twinge of pain, it was fine. She could leave when Nimue returned. She didn't have a clue where she would go. Home, a different town, or stay in Black Hollow?

"I need you to run an errand."

Tamlic's unexpected voice made her jump. "Excuse me?"

"Yosef gets up early to buy the flour, eggs, and everything else we need from Odds and Ends on the day, but since he hasn't been here... Well, we're close to running out. There's enough for another batch but no more. We might end up having a lot of annoyed customers. Most of them are farmers who'll come equipped with pitchforks." The gnome wriggled his nose. There was a smudge of flour underneath his left eye and a slightly panicked expression on his face. "The shop is down the street. You can't get lost. If we need to, we'll put the sign up in the window, even if this is his fault. It would serve him right if we lost money." He grumbled something about his docked wages.

"They wouldn't really come with pitchforks, would they?"

The corner of his mouth kicked up. "I don't want to risk it, do you?"

"No, it's okay. I'll head out." She picked up the crutch, tucking the wider top part underneath her arm. Since it was probably her fault he wasn't in to begin with, picking up the needed supplies was the least she could do. "It'll be nice to see the town. Don't worry, Tamlic, I'll be back before you know it."

"Take a few pieces of gold out of the till," Tamlic said as the kitchen door closed behind him.

Butterflies took up residence in the pit of her stomach. She hadn't left the bakery since she arrived in town. Everyone had been nice to her, and Bugrush hadn't made another appearance. Hadn't Yosef said something about reporting the incident to the guard? Ayako couldn't remember. She tried hard not to linger on the incident. She didn't have a clue as to why he had tried to grab her in the first place. *What did he call me, the bright lady?* Had he planned on selling her into slavery or worse? The thought made her shudder.

With her free hand, she picked up the basket he

used and went in search of Odds and Ends. A few customers who manned the stalls waved at her as she walked through the crowd. She smiled as she continued her trip, politely refusing the fish one of the sellers thrusted at her. The smell awful.

"Maybe another day, Saul."

The elderly man with wild white hair grinned at her, his mouth full of broken teeth or gaps.

A little girl, with black curls and a dirty face, rushed toward her with a bunch of flowers in her hand. She held them up. "Flowers, for a copper?"

Ayako shook her head. "They're very beautiful, but I'm afraid I don't have the coin to spare."

The girl didn't answer, instead rushing off and disappearing back into the crowd.

Odds and Ends wasn't a big building. And even with the sign worn by bad weather, she could still make out the words. She lifted her hand to push the door open, but something made her reach for her coin pouch. The comfortable weight at her hip had vanished. Frantic, she patted at her waist. Could the bag have moved with the belt she wore?

Dread filled her then annoyance. The little girl had robbed her—a distraction while her accomplice cut her purse free. Clever. A part of her would have been mildly impressed, but, instead, anger rolled inside of her like a ball of fire. The girl might have been desperate for the money, but the coin wasn't hers to give. What if they thought she stole the money herself? She stepped away from the building, with the crutch firmly underneath her arm, she went in search of the girl.

Short and with an almost supernatural ability to disappear in a crowd, Ayako didn't think she'd be easy to find. She kept her eyes peeled for any child who appeared suspicious. One darted from a gentleman and then down into an alleyway. Ayako hobbled after him.

When he entered Delectable Bites, she wasn't behind the counter. He'd half expected to see her wiping down the counters and humming to music only she could hear. He glanced behind him at the sign in the window. The one they put out when they were closed. Odd. There was still an hour to go. The kitchen door opened, and Tamlic glared at him. The gnome wasn't even vaguely intimidating, red in the face and sweat on the brow. Yosef had seen scarier tomatoes.

"And where have you been?"

He met his glare with one of his scowls. "Last time

I counted, gnome, I'm the boss. Not you. Or would you like me to dock your pay some more? Where is she?"

Tamlic frowned, and Yosef's heart took a one-way trip to the soles of his feet. Had his outburst scared her away?

"I was kind of hoping you might have bumped into her. She hasn't come back yet."

"Where is she?"

"We sent her out for supplies. The ones *you* should have gotten this morning and we needed." His tone grew defensive. "She should be back by now. I thought you were her."

He didn't bother to argue with him. Instead, he ran out onto the streets. He never reported Bugrush for attacking her. He'd had every intention to do so, but somehow, it'd slipped his mind. The beast of a man wasn't known to him, and Yosef didn't spend time outside the bakery. Was the orc a permanent fixture in town, or did he have friends? If she went out by herself, believing she was safe, she wouldn't have been on guard for him. He berated himself as he made his way to Odds and Ends.

Sitting on a chair near the entrance to his shop, Silvertongue glanced up from his activity of packing the pipe in his hand. "Yosef, you're on a late run."

"Have you seen a girl? She would have come here to get my things. Black hair. Green eyes. Pretty. Conservatively dressed." The words rushed out of his mouth, as if they had a life of their own. He kept an eye out for her. Maybe she got caught up in the new sights of the town? She hadn't had time to explore the area since she arrived.

Silvertongue shook his head. "Can't say I have."

Not waiting for more, he turned on his heels again and went from shopkeeper to shopkeeper. But some had already packed up for the day. None of the ones he questioned had seen her. *Where is she?* "Hey, is the information worth anything? I mean, if I know someone who's seen her?"

He glanced down at a little girl. Her face was dirty, and she had a headful of tight black curls. Her tight-fisted hands destroyed the flowers she carried. "Do you know something?"

She bit her bottom lip, which had started to quiver.

Kneeling, he got eye level with her. "She's important to me. You tell me what you know, and I'll give you a gold piece. You have my word, even if it doesn't mean much to you. I've got to find her."

She pointed at an alleyway. "The last time I saw

her, she was heading that way. It was a while ago."

There had to be more to the story, but he didn't have time to hear it. "Get the gold piece from Delectable Bites. Tell them Yosef sent you. Also, to give you some bread."

He ran for the alleyway. He should have told the others where he was going for the day, but how was he supposed to explain that he'd planned on seeing a goblin and begging for her forgiveness? Nobody but her would have believed him. He should have been able to get there and back in a decent time, but Elsbeth had been as stubborn as he thought she might be.

She hadn't been bothered by his need to atone, so she hadn't taken the envelope. But he had said he planned on visiting every week until she took it. Until she granted him the one thing he wanted. Forgiveness. If anyone found out he was torn up by the death of his former party members, they wouldn't have believed it. The only person who knew was Ayako, and she was now missing.

He turned the corner and stopped. A black shadow lay on the ground. "Ayako!"

He ran to her side, rolling her over and holding her in his arms. Her head lolled back, her hair pooling on the ground. Gingerly, he touched her neck, a place he should feel her heartbeat. He found the tell-tale thump there but discovered something else as well. A black mark at the base of her neck. Scales. Something had happened in the alleyway, and all he focused on was getting her away to someplace safe. He'd question the scales later. He stood up, carrying her in his arms.

He glanced around the alleyway. *Why did she come here?* His gaze narrowed on a spot on the ground. A black smudge and he breathed in deeply, trying to place the scent.

Something burnt.

"Yosef?"

He glanced down at her into green eyes he'd thought he might not see again. He placed a kiss on her forehead. "I'm here. It's going to be okay. Let's get you back to the bakery."

Unshed tears made her eyes shimmer like green pools. She clutched at her stomach, the pain she felt visible on her face. "I didn't mean to do it. I didn't think I could. I was so scared."

He walked out of the alleyway, carrying her. He didn't consider himself to be a strong man, but in this moment, he could have carried her anywhere. "What did you do?"

She clutched the front of his robes, her face full of

fear and revulsion. "I killed him."

Chapter Nine

Her grip on the front of his robes didn't lessen in the slightest; if anything, her knuckles turned white from the strain. He said something, but, completely trapped in her thoughts, the words didn't reach her. The memory of how she'd hobbled into the alleyway and how it was a dead end where Bugrush waited for her. The street kids worked for him, used to trap her. He grabbed her, ripping at her clothes. She remembered him saying she shone so bright and how he could get a lot of coins for her.

"Is she alright?"

She didn't move her head from his chest. Answering questions was the last thing on her mind. They wouldn't understand. A monster. A freak. Yosef ignored them, taking her upstairs. She noticed he took her to his room. "Can you walk?"

She nodded mutely.

He let her down next to the bed, and she sat, letting go of his robes. "I'll be right back."

Panic swelled in the pit of her stomach, but she pushed the terror down. His room was a safe space.

After a minute, he reappeared and sat next to her. "They're making you a drink."

As soon he spoke, Ayako burst into tears. She curled up next to him, holding on to him like her life depended on it. He rubbed her arm, the movement stilted and unsure. "Can you tell me what happened?"

She didn't know what to say, would he hate her?

"Did he hurt you?"

She wordlessly touched her shoulder where he'd grabbed her.

"I'll kill him." The dark words spoken with a certainty scared her.

She cried more. He made to move away from her, but she tightened her grip on him. "Don't leave me, please."

He brushed her hair off her naked shoulder. There was the barest moment where she froze before pulling away from him. Ayako slammed her hand over her scales. Bugrush grabbed her, tearing at her clothes and the buttons holding the neckline close. There was no way Yosef could have missed them. She glanced at him horrified, scared about his impending reaction.

"You're part dragon, aren't you?"

She shot up from his bed, darting away and running for the door. A hand on her wrist stopped her.

The power whirled in the pit of her stomach again, and she tore away from him, twisting her face away as the green mist gushed out of her mouth. Exhausted, she collapsed onto the floor. The mist didn't do any damage, but if it touched flesh, it ate away, leaving nothing but a black charred smug. Ayako put her hands to her face as the tears came. Was he was going to leave her here?

He knelt in front of her, and with her free hand, she waved at him. "Stay away. I don't want to hurt you."

Yosef sighed. "Take some deep breaths and try to calm down. You're safe here, you know I wouldn't hurt you. So, I need you to focus on the sound of my voice and breathe. Can you do that for me?"

He hadn't run from her, or pointed a finger and cast a spell to kill her on the spot. Those were good signs. After a few unsteady breaths, the crying stopped. His hand on her shoulder helped to centre her. The simple touch brought her back to the bedroom and away from the mental prison of the alleyway. There wouldn't be a day when she wouldn't remember what happened to her, but Yosef somehow pushed those unpleasant memories away. Something which should have been impossible.

She glanced up at him. "How can you look at me like that?"

He appeared confused. "Like what?"

"Like I'm not a monster?"

"A silly question, don't you think? Did you tell me I cared about monsters?"

"But I killed someone."

"If that's the measure of a monster, then I'm farther down the proverbial rabbit hole than you. I'm assuming you already knew you were half dragon?"

She sat on the floor, crossing her legs and not caring how her dress would be creased. He sat opposite her then removed his robe to reveal a pair of trousers and an off-white tunic. Almost like everyone else. "My mother. I get it from her side, but I've never done anything like that before. I shouldn't be able to."

"Spewing acid."

She wrinkled her nose at the description.

He shrugged. "An adept description of what you did."

"I know," she replied defensively. "Half-breeds don't have any real power; we inherit the visible markings." She gestured at her neck. "But none of the abilities tied to them."

Yosef rubbed his chin, studying her. "Yes, you said

that. All I can think is your reaction was a defensive mechanism. Something kicked in when you were in dire need."

"So, if I keep calm, it won't happen again?"

"I'm not sure. Possibly."

Where was the anger or the reaction of grabbing a sword to run her through with? Nimue said he hated anything with scales and he had every right, but he sounded almost reasonable. "Why aren't you trying to kill me?" A stupid question, and one she didn't want an answer to but asked anyway.

"Would you like me to?" He cocked an eyebrow.

She quickly shook her head, before realising her dress was still torn, and she held the front to her body.

Yosef leaned forward, reaching out behind her and draping his robes over her shoulders. "I'm assuming the black smudge was the orc?"

She nodded.

"He might have people who are going to search for him."

She made to stand up, but he grabbed her hand, keeping her on the wooden floorboards with him.

"Where do you think you're going?"

"I don't want to get anyone in trouble. I should go." She glanced down at their hands; his long fingers nearly covered hers completely. "I thought I could have a normal life, but I can't. I should go home."

He still didn't let her go.

"Yosef?"

"You didn't mean any harm, and you were protecting yourself. If you hadn't, it could have ended badly for you."

"I killed someone." Her breath caught on the word, as though all the air in her body vanished. She sat on the floor, utterly deflated. There was a soft knock before the door opened and revealed a guilt-ridden Tamlic. In his hand was a cup, the insides steaming with whatever it contained.

"I'm sorry, girl. I shouldn't have sent you out by yourself." He walked over to them and handed the cup to Ayako, who promptly put it next to her then gave the gnome a hug.

"You didn't know what would happen. Neither did I, but I'm here now. I'm okay." The gnome was resistant, and he awkwardly patted her on the shoulder.

"I'm glad you're okay." He pulled away and left the room.

Yosef laughed softly. "I don't think I've ever seen him so bashful before. I believe you've broken my gnome."

Ayako picked up the cup. She breathed deeply, amazed by the rich aroma. "What is this?"

"A special concoction of my own making. Shavings of chocolate, a touch of milk, and hot water. It'll help to soothe your nerves. Then you can tell me what happened." As they stayed on the floor, she tried to get her thoughts in order. She sipped the sweet hot liquid and fought against the urge to moan in delight. The taste was rich and sweet, the milk foamy, and she licked her top lip. She'd never tasted anything like this before.

"What do you think?"

"You should add this mixture to the menu."

"And risk having more customers?" He smiled at her. "I'd rather keep this little secret to myself."

"Well, I'm honoured you shared it with me." She held the cup tightly. "I was pick-pocketed. I noticed before I went into Odds and Ends. A girl stopped me, trying to sell flowers. I thought maybe it was her or someone she worked with, so I searched for her." She glanced down into the dark depths of her drink. "I didn't want you to think I stole it."

"Never would have occurred to me, not in your nature." He replied with a certainty she automatically believed.

"I wish I knew that." She sipped at the drink. "A young boy ran down an alleyway." Her chest tightened. "I followed...straight into a dead end. He was there, waiting for me." She didn't want to go on but she pushed on. "I think the kids worked for him or he hired them to get me to go in the alleyway."

"Then he attacked you?"

She nodded. "He laughed." Ayako closed her eyes. "Such a horrible sound. He knew he had me trapped. Nobody was coming to my rescue. I ran the best I could." She glanced up. "Even if I knew it was pointless. No blade in my boot, just me and him. He grabbed me, spun me around, and tore my dress. Everything happened so fast. I couldn't even scream."

A steely glare lit his gaze. She had seen him upset, caught up in emotions he couldn't face or admit to, but this? He gritted his teeth, and his hands clutched in tight fists. "You burnt him."

"Not that simple. One minute, he was there, looming over me and next, he was a mess on the cobbles. I didn't mean to but..." She let out a shuddered breath.

"He didn't leave you a choice. If you hadn't defended yourself, I would have killed him for hurting you." He sounded completely serious, and he took her hands into his. "I knew as soon as you left, you walked around with a target on your back. This is my fault, I should have reported the attack to the guards earlier, but I forgot. Ayako, please forgive me."

Her mouth opened then she closed it with an almost audible snap. "Don't be ridiculous. This isn't your fault."

"How about you stop blaming yourself and I'll do the same? Neither of us suspected this might happen but it's over."

"Even if I'm half dragon?"

He brought their hands up to his mouth and placed a kiss on their intertwined hands. Her breath caught in her throat, as heat swept over her. His lips were incredibly soft against her skin. "You're safe, Ayako. That's all that matters."

Chapter Ten

He waited for her to fall asleep before he left. It would have been easier if he'd put her in her own room, but the idea didn't sit well with him. She was still scared, and leaving her alone wasn't a good idea, especially if she woke in a panic. She might not feel it right now, but she was incredibly lucky to be alive, all due to her dragon heritage. She'd saved herself. The incident had ended with the remains of a dead body on the ground but better Bugrush than her.

Before Yosef left, he selected the book about the races from his bookshelf and carried the tome downstairs. He needed coffee and something to eat.

Tamlic and Catlo glanced up from their workstation as he entered the kitchen. "How is she doing, boss?"

Yosef could have been angry at the gnomes for sending her out for supplies. Unfortunately, the fault lay as much with him as them—in this case even more so. "An impossible question to answer. She broke down when I found her."

"What about the orc who attacked her?"

"Yeah." Catlo thumped a large rolling pin against his open palm. "Do you want us to find him and break his legs?"

Tamlic smiled cruelly. "Don't worry. It could be an accident."

She'd become a part of the dysfunctional family at the bakery. Yosef didn't think it possible, but she'd endeared herself to the gnomes quickly. Two years and he'd never become friends with them. She'd won them over in a week, probably because Ayako was a good person and the gnomes could smell bullshit from a mile away.

If she wanted them to know about her heritage, it would be up to her. Half-breeds were considered dangerous, and people acted out of fear rather than common sense.

"He ran away. She doesn't know where he went." At least there wasn't a body left behind. There wasn't even enough for the guards to identify the black smudge as the former orc. "She's resting in my room now. I'll man the counter tomorrow. There's no need to wake her; she should rest."

The gnomes shared a pointed look.

"What?"

"You've never worked the counter before." Catlo

rubbed his jaw. "Do you even know how?"

"I'm sure I can handle a day or so before Nimue gets back." He boiled the water and used some of the coffee beans he prepared earlier. Then a touch of sugar to take out some of the bitterness. "I need to do some research. I'll see you gentlemen in the morning." He wedged the book under one arm and picked up a slice of cake, putting it on a plate. As the door swung closed behind him, he caught snatches of conversation.

"Did he knock his head?"

"He's never called us gentlemen before."

Tamlic scoffed. "I guess girly is a good influence on him. You wouldn't believe what I saw in his bedroom."

Yosef went to his office and sat behind his desk, sorting out placements for the book on the stand, cake, and cup. Everything had its place. A part of him still believed that the world needed order, but Ayako was a hurricane who'd changed things he hadn't realised needed to be changed. An act he thought impossible.

He took a bite of the cake, making a mental note the sponge could be fluffier and a hint of vanilla would add much needed sweetness, then flipped the book open. Dragons. There were several entries, based mostly on colour. Each held different abilities, and, judging from her black scales, her linage drew from black dragons. They weren't any rarer than their brethren, but they were still near extinction. They were acid based, meaning they didn't blow out fire as a rule but a green mist incredibly toxic when in contact with skin. They were immune to poisons; thankfully, her ability shouldn't hurt her. Half-breeds were rare because frankly, what man thought it was a good idea to pursue a relationship with a dragon? Like any interaction with a dragon, they ended one way. A very final death rather than a romance.

He moved his finger anticlockwise, using the tiniest hint of power to move the spoon. A clever trick, one mainly used for show. He leaned back in his chair, picked up the cake, and continued to eat. Every now and then, he would wave his hand and change the page. He didn't know who Bugrush worked for or if he was a solo player. Would he have someone knocking on his door in the morning, seeking revenge? If they somehow linked the death of the unfortunate orc to the woman who slept in his bed. It would be a terrible idea for everyone involved.

The only safe place for her was out of Black Hollow. Far away from repercussions that might come searching for her. It would be selfish of him to ask her to stay, knowing the target on her back hadn't truly gone away. He could keep her safe, but he couldn't always be with her. To trade one cage for another. It wasn't fair for anyone. Even if he liked her more than he should.

Ayako rolled onto her side and took in the sights around her. The room Yosef created for her was bare bones. Not a single trace of personality. A temporary haven at best but one she would eventually have to leave.

His room was different. The blankets, blues and purples, were soft underneath her hands. A bookcase full of books with scrolls in large baskets on either side. He kept paintings on the walls, abstracts with soft yet vibrant colours. She'd been in his room before, but today was the first time she'd paid attention to the trappings within. It told her a lot about the man asleep on the wooden chair, with his legs outstretched in front of him. On the floor by his feet lay a book, and she took the blanket with her, wrapping the softness around her shoulders. She needed to change her clothes, but first, she knelt, opening the book. An encyclopaedia of races. Yosef was curious to find out more about her. A good sign. He wanted to know more, not try to kill her, even if he had already said he didn't plan to. As soon as the thought crossed her mind, she dismissed it. He could have hurt her when she slept, but he hadn't.

She could trust him.

She replaced the book on the shelf before she touched his cheek. His skin was rough against her palm, stubble. She caressed it, intrigued by the sensation. Her father had a beard, but his was thick and full. The wizard simply hadn't taken the time to shave. He stirred underneath her touch. "Yosef?"

He opened his eyes, brown orbs which watched her intently. "Hmmm?"

"I'm going back to my room to get changed. You can get into your bed. The chair can't be comfortable."

"I've slept in worse places." The wizard shook himself. "What's the time?" He stretched, and Ayako swore she heard bones crack. She liked the way he looked at the moment. The robe was very regal and made him appear unapproachable, but the simple trousers and collarless shirt suited him. She hadn't moved her hand from his shoulder; it hadn't escaped her notice touching him brought her a sense of calm.

"The morning light has made an appearance. The hours still early."

He stood. "Why are you awake?"

Samantha Allard

She let her hand drop to her side.

"I'm conditioned to wake up at ungodly hours. A habit I haven't been able to break." She kept the blanket wrapped around her shoulders. She wore an underdress with thin straps but served its job well, keeping her mostly covered. She didn't run the risk of flashing anything at Yosef, thankfully. It would have been an embarrassment she wouldn't have been able to live with.

Yosef stared at her.

"What?"

"I'm sorry, this might be intensely personal for you, but can I see your scales?"

She froze. Other than her parents, nobody else had seen them. "Why?"

"Do you remember when you told me Bugrush said, you shone brightly?"

She nodded.

"I was thinking about it last night, and I would like to test my theory. If you allow."

She pulled her hair over her shoulder. Yosef stepped closer, and, without much thought, she rested her forehead against his chest. Nobody touched her scales but her, and she didn't have a clue to how it might feel.

"I'm going to touch you."

"Thanks for the warning." She nearly jumped out of her skin as he touched the nape of her neck. A spark shot through her. A sensation she hadn't been expecting at all. It travelled all over her body, before resting in the pit of her stomach.

"Are you okay?" he asked, obviously concerned. "Did I hurt you?"

She shook her head. There was something intensely comforting about being close to him. "You've got cold hands."

"My apologies. I should have heated them first; I'm going to cast a spell called Detect Magic. I want to see if you're setting off a magical beacon. Do you trust me?"

She pulled away slightly, glancing up at him. Her hands on his chest. "Of course."

The barest pressure on her neck, and she was leaning into him. He muttered some words, and a warmth spread through her, down her neck and the curve of her spine. She shivered. "They really are quite beautiful." He touched her scales with the softest of pressure. Her breath caught.

"Thank you," she replied breathlessly. "I've never really seen them before. They are in a difficult place.

My mother always said they were pretty."

For a second, they stayed in the same position and could have been the only ones in the world. The wizard and the half dragon. The moment held a magic all its own. Damn, did she have feelings for him? As soon as the thought passed through her mind, she stepped away from him, confused. No, she couldn't. Any attraction to him would be insane.

He watched her with an unreadable gaze. And she found it hard not to stare at him—like something inside of her pulled them together. She couldn't read him, her empathy completely useless in the moment, like Yosef had erected a mental shield around his thoughts.

He couldn't feel the same way. How could anyone love someone when they were a part of the species which murdered his friends? She tried her best to ignore her thoughts. If she started to feel something now, it would be harder to leave.

"Did they ping? My scales?"

Yosef nodded. "Maybe Bugrush didn't know what you were and only got the strong magical reading. He really didn't strike me as someone with enough brain cells to cast a spell himself. Meaning, he might know a wizard who prepared an item to aid him with the task.

Maybe he thought you had something on you worth stealing?"

Nice to believe, but he didn't sound convinced. "What do you think?"

He shrugged. "Not possible to question him now. A fact in our favour. If he worked by himself, then nobody will come looking for him."

"But if he worked for someone and he doesn't come back? Then they'll know to come after me. Yosef, I can't stay. I need to leave before the town wakes up and people come searching for him." She had enough time to change her clothes and gather her things.

"Ayako."

"I can't stay." She gave him a hard stare. "I won't be the reason any of you get hurt."

"I'm a little insulted you think I can't defend myself. I'm not some hapless mortal. I'm a wizard. I've fought more monsters than I can count and walked away from those encounters. A few townsfolk don't scare me."

She fought against the urge to smile. There he was. The arrogant male wizard she knew.

"And what about the others? Tamlic and Catlo? Can they fight? Is it fair to ask them? I'm the one who killed him, Yosef. Now, I really need to change my clothes." She closed her eyes, rubbing the bridge of her nose. "I can't keep borrowing Nimue's clothes. I should have brought more things with me."

"Nimue would want you to take the clothes. I know they aren't your usual style, but we really don't have time to shop. She said she left them in the drawers since the spare room doesn't have a wardrobe."

Hiding the scales would be more difficult, but maybe she could wear her hair down or something? She admired the elf's style, but she doubted the low necklines and puffy sleeves would suit her. "It's certainly better than nothing."

"I'll see you downstairs."

Although nice that he wasn't going to argue with her, it was also odd. He wasn't a man who accepted things he didn't agree with. She frowned then went to her room. Going in search of the clothes Nimue had left her would give her time to figure out how to say goodbye.

Chapter Eleven

She'd had a rough couple of days, arguing with her wasn't going to work. Unfortunately, if she thought he was going to drop the subject and let her run out the door by herself, she was very wrong. When she went to change her clothes, Yosef opened his cupboard and pulled out clothes that, two years ago, he'd sworn he would never wear again. When he was finished, he readjusted his collar and retrieved his staff, left by the door.

Tamlic was visible behind the counter, wiping the heavy oak down and using a stool to reach places his short statue wouldn't allow. The gnome shot him a curious glare before his eyes widened. He'd never seen him in his adventuring garb. The walking boots were made from worn leather. His long grey woollen tunic was covered by a heavy dark-blue cloak, and he attached a leather belt around his waist. Yosef didn't believe in many gods, but he wore the amulet of the LightBrighter more out of habit than devotion. The oak staff he carried was three branches twisted together with magic and opened at the very top to cradle the blue sapphire in the centre. The gem was used as focus for the more advanced spells he knew, but he hoped he wouldn't need them.

"You're a little overdressed for greeting customers."

He smiled, bracing himself for the argument to come. "Nimue will be back tomorrow. You'll be fine for the day, but if I come home and this place is in a worse state than when I left? You'll be working for free until the debt is clear. Do I make myself clear?" He'd never left the gnomes in charge. But he worried about Ayako, so he had no choice but to make an exception.

Tamlic snorted. "I'm not a youngling, lad. I'm sure we'll manage. Where are you going?"

"Ayako is leaving town for a little while. I'm going to travel with her."

There was a creak from the stairs behind him. If Tamlic appeared surprised or shocked when he saw him, seeing her robbed him of all his senses. Yosef turned around and stopped himself short of letting his own jaw drop open. The dress Nimue left for her ended near the knee and was slightly less modest than the one she preferred. The leggings probably belonged to her but matched the rich blue of the dress perfectly. Her dark hair was down, a deliberate choice to help

hide the scales on her neck, he decided. She wasn't
paying them any attention, busy fastening the clasp
holding the cloak together.

Tamlic whistled underneath his breath. "You're
borrowing Nimue's clothes, lass?"

"It's not the first time I've worn something of
hers," she replied, sounding defensive. "I thought this
one was best to travel in. Guess I'm lucky we're close in
size." She glanced up and stopped on the step. Her
gaze swept over Yosef's attire. "Why are you dressed
like that?"

"I'm dressed for travel. Did you think you'd be
going by yourself?" He walked into the kitchen to sort
out rations. He didn't know where she came from
originally, but the trek couldn't be hard or difficult to
travel to since she arrived in Black Hollow in one
piece.

He wrapped up some bread and dried meat in a
cloth. They could hunt for food if need be or drop by
the general store to find more things. Then he took out
two empty water bags; they would need to fill them at
the well before they left Black Hollow. He had made a
solemn promise to himself he would never go
adventuring again. He didn't know why he'd kept
things from the time.

Maybe he was sentimental.

Catlo hadn't said anything at the sight of him. Instead, he sighed and resumed his job of kneading dough. The door opened behind Yosef, with enough force he would have jumped at the sound if he hadn't been expecting it. Catlo went white and darted out of the room.

He didn't turn around, but he suspected Ayako might be a little angry. "How did you interpret me keeping you safe, with you coming with me?"

He didn't turn around. "This is me keeping you safe. We have no idea if anyone is going to come after you. You don't have any real magic; the acid mist is a reflex but not anything you can control." He finished packing, pulling the string to close it. "You could walk out this door, and maybe you'll get home without getting into trouble. Or you could walk out this door, get out of town, trip over a branch, and hurt your ankle."

"Your faith in me is overwhelming."

Her tart tone brought him around to face her.

"The forests are not safe for unwary travellers. I doubt you'd be inclined to travel by horse and cart, so you'd probably try and walk. If you don't want to risk us, you won't risk strangers because it's who you are.

And you're being incredibly stupid."

She crossed her arms—an odd sight to see her in Nimue's clothes and angry. The half dragon was even-tempered and shy. Very unlike how he would have pictured someone with such a complicated linage.

Her hair hanging in silky waves softened her facial features, and, with her petite frame, she wasn't intimidating in the slightest. But the glare on her face made him question those assumptions. Yosef wasn't wrong as a rule, but he found it refreshing to see Ayako had a backbone. The pink tinge to her face became redder, and he realised he was staring at her. Either uncomfortable or she was getting angrier.

In that moment, he would have gladly gone up against a troll than argue with her any longer.

"Stupid. Is that really what you think I'm being?"

"Yes. You're making a stupid decision. You believe you're being noble by keeping us safe. It's sweet. But it is also obvious you have terrible luck. How long were you in town before you were attacked?" He didn't wait for her to answer. "I have years of experience in adventuring, and the spells I know will keep us both safe. Accept my help, Ayako, or be prepared for me to follow you to your home to make sure you arrive safely."

She stomped her foot. "Why are you being so stubborn?"

"I think the real question is, why are *you* being stubborn?" He closed the distance between them, the sound of his staff loud on the wooden floorboards. He hadn't carried a staff for a while, but it was an extension of his body. A part of him. Standing opposite her, he realised her boots added an extra inch of height, and they were close to eye level.

"I want to keep you safe. How can I accomplish that, knowing you coming with me won't end well?"

"I'm not going anywhere unless I'm with you. The more we argue, the less time we have to get out of here before someone comes searching for you. Then we might have to fight our way out." He lightly touched her shoulder. "Please, stop arguing with me on this."

She bit her bottom lip, her expression conflicted. It would give the gnomes something to gossip about with Nimue when she returned. The elf probably wouldn't be incredibly happy with him, either, but the decision was for the best. He would keep the half dragon safe, deliver her to her formidable mother, and utter the word *goodbye*.

Yosef hired two horses, taking the black stallion for himself. The beige-and-white mare was hers, her sweet nature and the way she nudged her hand endeared her to Ayako quickly. Neither of them had names, but she touched her snout and settled on Buttercup. Yosef rolled his eyes, but she ignored him. There was a large forest in the distance, and he said it would take an hour to reach. They travelled on the roads used by merchants and those who transported travellers; the same road she'd taken to reach Black Hollow. A slightly beaten path with loose rocks and overgrown weeds and wildflowers. It was only when they reached the forest, he spoke again.

"You shouldn't name a horse."

She frowned. "Why?" Ayako hadn't enjoyed the first time she travelled this way. The cart she arrived on had been pulled by two large horses and guided by a man called Damich. The older man, with tufts of white hair above his ears, had travelled with a large crossbow across his lap. He hadn't spoken to her and kept a keen eye on the dark forest.

"You run the risk of creating a bond. Horses generally don't live awfully long with adventurers." He said the words so matter-of-factly, it sent a shiver down her spine. "There are monsters and beasts who call this place home. Giant spiders and wolves to name two. And I'm sorry, but if I have to choose between us or the horses, I'm picking us."

Ayako rubbed the horse's neck, her mane coarse underneath her hand. "Ignore him. I'm sure the wizard doesn't know the meaning of looking on the bright side. Don't listen to him."

He snorted. "I prefer the word realist."

The bags he packed were attached to the saddles to make sure they were secure. They decided not to take the crutch. Instead, he handed her a long staff. She could use it to help her walk if she needed or as a makeshift weapon. Ayako hoped she wouldn't need it. His own staff was attached to his bag, but he would be able to remove it quickly if he needed. A wizard with his staff was a dangerous thing. Her wooden staff was only suitable as a makeshift club to bonk someone over the head with. In her boot was the knife, but, in a rush, she might not be able to pull the blade free. She couldn't rely on the acid mist to keep herself safe since she didn't know how to make her recessive dragon ability work.

The empathy was a lost cause. The ability wouldn't help in a fight.

"Do you know where Dromlach Dragan is?"

"The Dragon's Spine? I've never been but it's by the Adrid Bluffs. You're from there?" It didn't surprise her he knew the translation. Yosef knew a lot of things or certainly spoke in a way nobody questioned his knowledge. "An ideal place for a dragon to settle. Plenty of mountains to shield her from the outside world."

She shrugged, a little annoyed he'd guessed the reason without any help. "My mother ages slower than mortals. She decided a long time ago to keep as much distance between her and others as possible. My home is a tiny cottage near the mountain range. I always thought the ground resembled rolling waves. The way the wind caught the strands of grass. There isn't a place like it in the world. At least nothing I've discovered, but I haven't been very far from home."

"Have you heard about the Waterfalls of the Sirena?"

She shook her head.

"The Sirena are a race of merpeople. Their scales are iridescence, pink, yellow, and blue constantly shimmering in the rays of the sun. When the sun is high, the water changes colours." A small smile tilted his lips. A good memory with the party he lost.

"Sounds beautiful. Why were you there?"

"The King of the region hired us to retrieve a golden ball left behind by his daughter in the area. The princess liked to hear the Sirena sing. She said she was attacked by a Karnack, a frog person he wanted us to kill. We didn't. It was a rare time we let a monster live. The daughter promised the frog person her friendship and broke the vow. I believe he still calls the waterfall his home. I haven't been there for years."

"It sounds beautiful."

The sun was low in the sky. This time of year, night fell early. She didn't know how long they had before they needed to camp for the night. Two hours, maybe four if they pushed. When Ayako left home, she travelled by horse with her mother until they reached the town of Rakare. Abel had been their family horse for a long time and had been trained not to bolt when her mother rode him. She rarely transformed into her dragon form, but the animals could still sense she was a predator. Rakare was a seaside town and one Ayako could have stayed at if she'd chosen to. Her mother left with the horse, and then she hired Damich to take her farther. The first time she left home, choosing to live a few hours away seemed counterproductive. A few days travelling by cart and she ended up in Black Hollow. And straight into trouble. She absentmindedly stroked Buttercup's flank. Her mother would be thrilled her only offspring had inherited some of her abilities.

Beltrix the Black was the best person to train her in control.

They travelled in silence. Ayako was happy for the respite. Yosef was a clever man; a million thoughts probably ran through his mind. She, on the other hand, was trapped in the past. The death of Bugrush. Panic and fear. Emotions she hadn't experienced much before arriving in Black Hollow. They twisted her stomach up in knots. She needed to keep herself in a happy mood or risk throwing up green mist which made flesh burnt, crisp and melt away. Wonderful.

She sneaked a look at him. He kept his gaze on the surrounding area. Trees cornered them in, and the late afternoon sun made the shadows even longer. She couldn't read his expression. Was it boredom or readiness for a battle she couldn't see? Was there really something in the forest wanting to gnaw on their bones?

She followed his gaze, trusting Buttercup would keep them on the path. She appeared more fidgety— maybe she could also sense something Ayako couldn't see. Anything could have been hiding in those shadows. "Is everything alright?"

Yosef probably expected her to say anything because, while her voice sounded impossibly loud breaking the silence, he barely jumped. "Everything's fine. I'm thinking about how much farther we should travel before we rest for the night."

"Is it a good idea to stop here?"

He shook his head. "Probably not, but we'll need to stop somewhere soon. Travelling at night is never a good idea. How ever did you manage to get to Black Hollow without getting in trouble?"

Ayako explained how she travelled with her mother and then a cart. It had been luck. A sentiment he echoed, annoying her slightly. Why did he have to agree with her? Because he didn't see her as anything other than a girl who needed to be rescued. An oddity but not an equal. She kept her thoughts to herself, but she couldn't ignore the fact the knowledge hurt.

They travelled for another hour, and then he directed them to a clearing. A circle of trees with a smaller circle of stones in the centre. A makeshift camp used by other adventurers. He swung his leg over the horse and jumped off. Ayako followed suit. The horses grazed on some overgrown weeds.

"Do we need to tie them up to a tree?"

Yosef shook his head. "No point. They know there are some dangerous things in this forest. Tying them up to a tree will leave them trapped with no means of escape. I'm not completely heartless." He muttered the last part so low she nearly missed it.

"I've never called you that."

"Never said you did. I'm going to collect some firewood. Stay here with the horses."

He took off with his staff, and Buttercup nudged against her side. She laughed, the sound impossibly loud in the wooded area. She caught sight of Yosef stopping, and, for a second, she hoped he might turn around. But, after a moment, he made his way deeper into the forest.

Chapter Twelve

There hadn't been much point in purchasing two horses. Yosef knew a lot of spells. A trait all well-learnt wizards possessed, but they could only use so many before exhaustion hit. He could have brought into existence a demonic steed, but the sight might have scared Ayako. They were summoned from the depths of the hell planes and lasted for six hours before they returned to their realm. He wasn't one to show off. Unnecessary spells, when a normal horse served the purpose and saved a higher-level spell for later, worked just as well.

The trip had mostly passed in silence. Ayako deep in thought and possibly still annoyed he decided to tag along. Yosef appreciated the silence. There was nothing to talk about and leaving him to focus on their surroundings. There were a lot of shadows cast by tall trees. Each one of them big enough to hide something behind the trunk or in the branches. The only time she babbled was when she was nervous, but she hadn't appeared nervous. She was worried. About him? Possibly. Yosef had promised to keep her safe. It was a little insulting she still didn't believe him.

One thing worrying him was her reluctance to talk about Bugrush. From experience, burying things was ill-advised. She helped to teach him the lesson after all.

He scooped up some twigs from the leafy ground. What on earth was he doing? Yosef didn't make a habit of questioning himself. He always had complete faith everything he did was the right choice. The only time he'd gone against his instincts was when they went to get the scales from the dragon, and the result of going against the feeling in his gut hadn't ended well for anyone. What about Ayako made him go against every inch of his being? An innocent, with a knack for getting into trouble. It didn't interest him in the slightest. He preferred his life quiet and uninteresting. Perfectly happy to invest time in new recipes. Ayako was dangerous but not in the way she thought. Yosef didn't want to play protector or guardian. The dark-haired beauty assaulted each one of his senses. Made him question himself and face his past mistakes without any judgement from her. A half dragon who didn't want revenge for one of her kind?

"And you like her. Simpler to admit the truth to yourself at least." The words gave him pause. He'd never said them out loud before. Doing so made his feelings real and something he didn't want to face. He quickly glanced around to make sure she hadn't followed him.

"No, you don't," he said to the empty forest.

In the end, he didn't want her death on his conscience. If he left her to her own devices, she wouldn't last five minutes. He'd never met someone who danced so close to misfortune.

He quickly picked up some more twigs and returned to the camp. Ayako had rolled out the bedrolls and was sorting through the rations. The horses were lying next to each other, staying close to her. She barely spared him a glance as he went about sorting the twigs, except to hand him a piece of flint she kept in her bag. He ignored her, instead, raising his hand, focusing the power inside of him. Ayako's eyes went wide as the tips of his fingers started to glow, and a tiny flicker of flame came off, igniting the brittle twigs. They crackled almost happily, and he sat down with a huff. The spell was simple enough, taking no real skill besides the talent to cast spells.

"What?"

"Nothing. I've never seen you cast spells before."

"I guess you don't have much experience with wizards, then?"

The Wizard of Black Hollow

"Mother can cast spells, but her magic is different. She's a mythical beast filled with magic and mystery." She sighed heavily and Yosef suspected it wasn't the first time she'd heard or spoken the words. "How is it possible a human can do the same magic?" Ayako reached into her bag, pulled out some bread, ripped the doughy offering in two, and handed half to him. She sounded generally interested.

"There are many theories to why humans ended up with the ability to cast spells." He bit into the bread; the nutmeg blend was one of his favourites. Ayako got comfortable, leaning against a fallen tree, her legs outstretched in front of her, her cloak wrapped around her, helping to fight the chill in the air.

"Which theory do you like the best?"

"You seriously want to know?"

She nodded.

He thought back to the lessons he had with Braxton. The old man was a romantic at heart and taught him about the history of magic. He remembered the times the man went off on a tangent, and ten-year-old Yosef glanced out of the window watching the world go by. "One theory I liked was how the races all lived on separate planes of existence for thousands of years. The elves discovered the magic to open portals, and they appeared in our realm. The leader of the elven expedition was a beautiful woman, Lady Adriana. She fell in love with King Edmund. Their children were the first half-breeds. Over the years, the lines between elf and human blurred, the magic carrying on through the lines."

"You're part elf?"

Yosef shrugged. "It's a theory passed down the lines for however long. Those of us blessed with magic probably have elven blood somewhere in our line. There are obviously others who can cast magic. Sorcerer's make pacts with demons or other higher beings for their magic. Druids worship the gods of the forest."

She was frowning.

"What?"

"Nothing, I have to admit, I'm surprised that's the one you like. You don't strike me as someone who enjoys a love story."

"What makes you come to that conclusion?"

She popped a piece of bread into her mouth, apparently mulling the answer over. "You're very practical. A loner who only keeps company because he doesn't have a choice. Don't get me wrong, you obviously care for people, even if you are loathed to admit it. I thought you would lean towards a practical story, not a union based out of love as a basis for wizards' powers."

She really thought that way about him? "I'm not made out of stone."

"I know you're not. I like seeing this side of you. I get the feeling a lot of people don't see it."

A rare feeling of rage swept over him. This was ridiculous. What about her made him spill his guts like that, like a spell? Yosef made a few gestures in the air, casting detect magic. The scales and her dragon heritage pinged, but there was something else, something barely there, beneath the surface. All magic had a unique taste, making it easy to distinguish the class where it originated.

"What are you doing?"

"I believe the correct question is, what are you doing?" He glared at her. "You're casting a spell."

Guilt washed through her, heat suffusing her face. The moment had been so pleasant and all she'd wanted. She'd chosen to put her life into his hands even though she worried he'd be hurt because of her. The empathy swept from her into him, as if it had a life of its own. "Not on purpose. I don't have any control."

"I hear the word from you a lot." He snapped his

fingers. "Empathy. You can use empathy, and you know you can." Yosef got to his feet, and Ayako followed suit. "I knew dragons had the talent, and I suspected you might have the ability but not the control." He stormed off. "It's bad manners to cast spells on those trying to help you."

She went after him, reaching for his arm, but he flinched, and she pulled her hand away. "I'm sorry. It's instinct. I don't even know how to make the ability work. I swear." She didn't want to see the expression on his face, his distrust. "Yosef, you know I can't control my abilities. It just comes to the surface. I wouldn't intentionally hurt you. All I've wanted to do was keep you safe by leaving. You're the one who wanted to come with me."

"You could have used the empathy to influence my decision, and I wouldn't have been the wiser."

"Yosef." Her eyes burnt, but she refused to cry in front of him.

"I've told you things I haven't told anyone." He raised his staff, his gaze narrowing. "My life would have been easier if we had never met to begin with."

The words hit her with a strength she didn't think was possible, and all the will of not crying in front of him fell to the wayside. "Do you really mean that?"

The Wizard of Black Hollow

From the corner of her eye, she caught sight of something moving. Her imagination played tricks on her. She rubbed her eyes, trying to get a clearer look, but the fire made the shadows appear even longer than normal.

"Get down!"

"Wait a minute, what?"

He roughly grabbed her arm and swung her around, so she was stood behind him. Ayako fought against the urge to grab the back of his cloak, leaving both of his hands free.

She risked a glance over her shoulder. The shadows moved. No, not moved...skittered. "We're surrounded. By what?"

He swore underneath his breath and muttered something about a rookie mistake. "We must have gotten their attention when we started arguing."

She'd left her staff by the fallen tree, too far to reach before a spider got her. She kept her gaze forward, catching the moment the hairy eight-legged beasts broke free of the tree line, the firelight illuminating them. Ayako had seen spiders before but nothing like this. Six-foot tall with dripping fangs—the stuff of nightmares, which she'd have for years if she lived to see the morning.

"How many do you have?" Yosef barked.

"Two too many." The nasty, shadowy things crawling toward her. The horses bolted, but the spiders barely spared them a glance. Perhaps the two of them, Ayako and Yosef, were the easiest meal. "Please, tell me you have a way out of this."

"Don't really want to take my eyes off these things, but I have an idea." He took her hand into his, a warm sensation as their palms touched.

She glanced over her shoulder as he softly spoke the words of another spell, but, like the last one, she didn't recognise it. The closest spider lurched for him, and she screamed before instinct kicked in. She spun them around, swapping places, and ended up facing Yosef, who was muttering the last part of the spell. His eyes were wide, his mouth dropped open, but she only had a moment to recognise it before the spider struck with one of its hairy legs. Moments played in torturous slow moments like the grains of sand trickling through an hourglass. For a brief second, a blissful numbness swept through her. Then a buildup of pressure as the leg tore through cloth and hit the flesh beneath. The pain hit; her legs buckled underneath her as her breath caught. Yosef grabbed her around the waist and dragged her through the portal as venom pulsated

The Wizard of Black Hollow

inside of her, turning her vision dark.

Chapter Thirteen

One minute, they'd been in the clearing. Spiders, with gnashing teeth, looming in on all sides. The firelight highlighted dripping fangs and many sets of eyes, each reflecting Yosef's focused expression as he tried to complete the spell. Wizards could cast many spells, but all of them required concretion. Break a wizard's focus and the spell was lost. The spider darted for him. He knew if the beast hit him, he would lose the spell. Of all the things he thought might happen next, he never would have guessed she'd swap places with him.

He saw the precise moment the spider hit her. The way her eyes widened and breath caught. In the next moment, the spell took shape, opening a bubble behind them, which he dragged her though then released with a *pop*. They were roughly a 100 ft. away on the battered road they travelled in on. Without a light, it wasn't easy to figure out their precise location. Portals were proved invaluable in close combat against many enemies. A higher-level spell, and one he wouldn't be able to cast again until he rested.

She slumped against his chest as the portal vanished. There wasn't time to assist her condition; they needed to get more distance between the spiders and themselves. He helped her to the leafy ground; her black hair made her skin appear almost ghost like. There was an inky blackness on the sleeve of his robe, her blood.

"Ayako, why did you do that? Out of all the things you've done, this was, by far, the most dangerous."

Her eyelids fluttered slightly. "You needed to complete the spell. I couldn't let you get hurt." Her eyes remained closed, her breathing laboured.

Spiders could travel at great speeds, and four of them had attacked them, so there was no telling how many more called the forest their home. He stood and started to conjure a demonic steed. Yosef pulled at the air with both hands, gathering up the invisible threads of magic which made up all things. The creature could only be summoned with magic and sheer force of will. There was some resistance. The creature fought against his will. The instilled panic of an injured Ayako played havoc with his focus.

Yosef gritted his teeth. "Listen to me, you blasted thing. I call and you answer. That's how this works."

Purple mists took shape in front of him. The steed

was nothing like the horses, its name an adequate way to describe something dragging its way out of the hell planes, with red eyes and purple smoke coming out of its snout. He picked up the still form of the half-dragon girl, positioning her near the steed's neck before he climbed up onto the beast as well.

Yosef lost count of time, all his focus on the horizon and the light growing bigger the closer they got. Town, city, or a home? He didn't care, only that he got there. She might have been manifesting dragon abilities, but there was no way of knowing if rapid healing was one of them. Also, her mother's race was immune to most, if not all poisons. He couldn't risk waiting to find out. Besides the words she spoke before he conjured the steed, she lost consciousness some time ago and hadn't regained it since. A rapid ride on a demonic horse wasn't the smoothest means of travel.

What had she been thinking? Why had she swapped places with him? He might have been about to take the hit and still complete the spell. She shouldn't have put herself at risk, not for him. *I didn't want you to get hurt.* That was what she said before she fell unconscious. She'd sacrificed herself to keep him safe. Even after he'd accused her of manipulating him.

I'm a jackass.

She had never given him a reason not to trust her. Then he'd latched on to her empathy as an excuse to put distance between them. Finally admitting to himself he had feelings for her, only to push her away at the earliest opportunity said more about him than her. She might not be able to control her talent, like breathing out the acid mist. The only difference was she'd known about it.

The precise moment she woke up, her body, lax and unmoving, suddenly stiffed. He brought the demonic steed to a halt. The creature snorted, scuffling the ground with its hooves.

"Ayako?"

"This is really uncomfortable."

He swung his leg over the steed and slid to the ground. Then helped Ayako, and, while she was a little unsteady on her feet, she kept them beneath her. He didn't let go of her, and she rested her head against his chest.

"What happened?"

"You got stabbed by one of the spiders, I'm taking you somewhere to get help. How do you feel?"

She glanced up at him. A fine layer of sweat covered her pale skin, and she was still shaking. "I think I'm fine. Are you okay?"

He had a hard time making out her features in the moonlight, but there was no way he could miss the concern in her voice. She was pure insanity in human form. How could she be thinking of him in a moment like this? In her current state? After they argued?

Why was he still fighting with himself?

He cupped the sides of her face with his hands and kissed her. She stiffened slightly, and, for a moment, he wondered if he'd made a mistake. But then she returned the kiss, relaxing against him. He broke the contact, bemused at her half-closed eyes and the small smile on her lips. "I'm sorry we argued. We're heading to the nearest town to see if you're alright. Also, we need to buy you some new clothes, you do have a gaping hole in the back of your dress."

"I really liked this dress." She sighed. "Okay, tell me all of this again when I wake up?"

He frowned. "Ayako, you are awake."

"Doubtful. I'm fairly sure you would only kiss me in my dreams."

He nearly laughed. Truer words had never been spoken. If he hadn't been scared of losing her, he might never have done it. "Come on. Let's get you back on and get you some help."

Ayako sat behind him, her arms around his waist and the side of her face resting against him. The wound on her back still hurt but nothing like when she was first stabbed. Her mother could heal from most injures. She remembered a time her mother cut her hand on a shard of glass and it had healed almost instantaneously. If she inherited the ability, it would certainly be useful. Especially since her poor decision-making skills always ended up with her hurt.

She closed her eyes, the feel of Yosef's heartbeat against her cheek a steady rhythm, bringing her a small amount of peace.

He brought the steed to a stop then pressed the slightest pressure on her hands. "We're here, Ayako. Let's see if we can get a cleric to heal you."

She reluctantly let him go, and he helped her off the steed. The beast neighed, as though bidding them farewell, and Yosef patted its snout before its body became wisp-like and it vanished back into the ether. Yosef put his arm around her waist, helping her keep her balance. Exhaustion swept over her. A long day without sleep and then being hurt? She ran on barely there reserves. She used sheer will to put one foot in front of the other.

"Can we afford a cleric? We both left our packs

behind. I only have a few coins in my pouch."

"Don't worry."

"Yosef?"

He sighed, and, for a second, it was like they'd never shared a kiss. Maybe the intimate moment hadn't meant the same for him, just relief she wasn't dead, and he didn't have to explain her body to her mother...who would burn him to a crisp if her only daughter ended up dead. "I always keep a few gold pieces on me, and if it's not enough, I can offer my skills as a wizard as payment for the debt."

It might have been the middle of the night, but there were still people on the street, stumbling from tavern to tavern. He enquired about the nearest temple. A few of them ignored him, but a woman with a shawl wrapped around her shoulders pointed out a simple courtyard with a round tower in the centre.

He rubbed his jaw. "Who's the God they worship?"

"The Lightbringer, but it doesn't matter. They won't turn anyone away for needing help. Are you okay?" The last part was directed at Ayako, who nodded.

"The downside of travelling through a forest where spiders call home."

The woman whistled. "You're lucky to be alive."

She scowled at her wizard before smiling at her. "Next time, choose who you travel with more wisely."

"If I hadn't travelled with him, I wouldn't be here at all," she replied defensively.

Yosef led her away toward the temple. "Not a good time to argue with the locals."

"But you've been keeping me safe." She yawned, and his grip tightened around her waist.

"You were stabbed by a spider. How safe am I keeping you?"

"You didn't use me as a human shield. You can't control every crazy impulse I have or see through." He ignored her mutterings.

Her injury wasn't his fault. There was no way he could have known she planned on doing something stupid, even if it appeared to be her automatic response to most situations. She didn't want to argue with him or think about the aching throb on her back. Instead, she focused on other, more complicated things. Should they talk about the kiss? Who should bring the subject up first? Should they pretend it never happened? Or should she ignore her first kiss as something given in the heat of the moment? Her head hurt. The world outside the Dragon's Spine was confusing. "What if the temple's closed?"

Yosef scoffed. "The temple is never closed. There's always at least a cleric or acolyte on the grounds who can help someone if needed. I can't tell you the number of times a temple saved me and the others in my party. They offer a place to rest and a supply of potions, if they have any to spare.

He pushed against the gate with a free hand, and it swung open. Flowers and herbs filled the courtyard, the smell intoxicating. The cleric's personal supply for the healing potions and tonic they sold. At the current hour, there wasn't anyone tending to the garden, but there was a faint light coming from the tower. She let him lead the way, not trusting her feet. His heavy knocks against the solid oak door didn't bring anyone, and when he tried the handle, it didn't turn.

"Wait a minute. Wait a minute," a male grumbled from the other side, the rattling keys following. "Does this one open the front door? This one? No, Cassandra put a speck of red paint on it, to distinguish from the others." Another rattle of keys. "No, not red, yellow. Cedric, you are going senile in your old age."

"I believe I've aged ten years waiting for this blasted thing to be opened," Yosef growled.

Ayako fought the urge to giggle. She blamed it on the exhaustion, but to see Yosef being kept waiting still amused her greatly.

The door swung open, and an elderly gentleman peered out at them over a pair of wire-rimmed glasses. His white hair revealed a glimmering bald spot on the very top of his head. "I'm sorry to keep you waiting." He glanced up at Yosef. "The hour is rather late, young man. The temple of the Lightbringer is currently closed."

"I would have never guessed by the fact the door was locked," he replied dryly. "My companion encountered a spider and was hurt. Can you get someone who can heal her? I'm worried the spider was poisonous. Most of them are after all."

"Oh my. How terrible. Please, come in both of you. I'll get one of the clerics." He hobbled off to a board on the wall with two lines of bells on it. "Who's on duty this evening? May or Christopher?" He tapped his bottom lip.

Yosef sighed heavily, and this time, she burst out laughing. He frowned down at her. "I'm sorry, I'm a little tired. It's been a long day."

"Any would be preferable," he told the old man. "Just ring a blasted bell."

"There's no reason for the attitude, son." Cedric peered at her over the rim of his glasses. "Your friend doesn't appear to be on her last legs." He reached for a bell and pulled. "Follow me. I'll take you to one of the treatment rooms."

She'd never been in a temple before. A large round, open space with a statue of the Lightbringer in the centre of the room. A circlet, representing the sun, adorned his dragon head. Benches had been placed around him. Places where the acolytes and clerics sat down and prayed? Slightly farther on the other side of the room were doors and a set of spiral stairs leading up to the floor above them. There were also plenty of bookcases stuffed with books.

Cedric led them into one of the rooms, revealing a bed covered by a white sheet. A small table and chair were pushed into one of the corners. There was a window, but there wasn't any time to glance outside as Yosef led her to the bed and helped her sit down.

"I really am feeling a lot better," she protested.

"Humour me."

A young woman rushed into the room, her cleric robes emblazoned with the symbol of her god in gold, swirling around her legs. Her sharp black bob was ruffled, as if she'd been woken from a deep sleep.

"I'm sorry about waking you, May, these kind folks are in need of a little aid."

She nodded. "It's not a problem, Cedric. What happened?"

Ayako let Yosef tell her everything. Thankfully, he didn't mention her dragon heritage. The Lightbringer might have been a dragon, but there was no telling how people would react to her interesting linage. The cleric walked around her and helped her take her cloak off. She pulled her hair to the side, trying to make sure the strands still covered her scales.

"I can see you were definitely hit, but there isn't much I can do to help. There's a scratch. You're incredibly lucky." The woman prodded her back, and she flinched. "There is some blood but still not enough damage to worry ourselves about. I'll get you some anti-venom tonic just in case." She patted Ayako's shoulder and smiled down at her. "Perhaps don't travel at night next time."

"I did tell her it was ill-advised." Yosef crossed his arms, his brow furrowed.

"Perhaps say it more forcefully next time? I'm going to bed," the woman announced. "Cedric, you know where the tonics are kept." She faced Ayako as Cedric left the room. "I'll check in on you in the morning. I really hate the night shift." Cleric May yawned as she walked unsteadily toward the door then turned to Yosef. "Keep an eye on her. The damage isn't nearly as bad as it could have been, but if the spider was poisonous, she's going to have a rough night."

Cedric finally made his way to the room and handed Ayako a small glass container of green liquid. "Drink."

She did as told, the viscous fluid coating her throat. She shuddered.

Yosef nodded thanks at Cedric as the old man hobbled out, and when they were finally left alone together, he sat next to her on the cot.

"I guess I inherited my mother's healing abilities as well."

"I guess you didn't know."

There wasn't really a question there. He might have doubted her about the empathy but not this. He slumped; his usual regal bearing vanished to reveal a much more human response. Like he'd been holding his breath and could now only just breathe again.

"Not really something I can test." She shrugged. "And the venom?"

"You're the daughter of a black dragon. They're immune to venoms and poisons. It's possible you've inherited that talent as well, but I'd prefer if we stay here until the morning. Just in case. Also, we need to buy you some new clothes in the morning. Can't have you going home in your current state."

She agreed. "My mother probably wouldn't let me explain before she burnt you to a crisp."

"Not the best way to make a first impression."

She lay down, resting her head against his lap. He draped her cloak over her. "I'm sure she'll like you."

He smiled down at her, brushing strands of hair from her eyes. "What makes you say that?"

"Because I like you." Ayako closed her eyes.

Chapter Fourteen

When Ayako fell asleep, Yosef went in search of Cedric and got a bedroll from him. He asked how much the treatment cost. Since the cleric hadn't needed to cast any spells, the price was much lower than he'd thought it would end up being. He promised to pay for the tonic in the morning then went back to the room.

She hadn't moved. The gentle rise and fall of her chest assured him she was alright. He rolled his cloak, using the heavy fabric as a makeshift pillow, and lay down, lacing his fingers together underneath his head as he stared at the ceiling. A kiss. He had kissed her, changing everything. He frowned. The kiss didn't have to change anything. He could still get her home and leave her there. Be perfectly happy with his bakery and not think of her again. Her smile. Laugh. The way her nose wrinkled when she thought about something.

Dammit.

He punched the makeshift pillow a few times and curled up onto his side, the bare wall filling his vision. He shouldn't have kissed her, but the relief she was okay had overwhelmed every ounce of common sense he possessed. To keep his feelings to himself and, if need be, deny them completely. She, on the other hand, barely thought about anything she did. Acting on instincts all her own. The opposite of him and his clinical way of viewing the world. In the moment of fight or flight, she'd thrown herself into the path of danger to keep him safe.

What would happen next?

He didn't like the uncertainty. A woman of chaos had effectively overturned his life completely. The only bright side? He and Ayako weren't being followed. Either Bugrush hadn't had any cohorts to begin with, or they didn't know she had killed their friend.

She was safe. He could leave if he wanted. The thing was...he didn't want to leave her.

Falling in love with a being of chaos. The gods were cruel.

He woke to someone nudging his shoulder. He opened his eyes to see Ayako smiling down at him. The light from the window made her skin glow, and she had tied her hair up, revealing the delicate curve of her neck. For a second, he couldn't do anything but stare up at her. She was beautiful. Vibrant. The seconds passed. Neither of them moving.

"Morning." She smiled, like she could read his mind.

He rubbed at his face. "What's the time?"

"Still early." She moved away. "We should leave now. The shops have started to open. I'll grab a dress then we can go."

"I'll need to pay the clerics first. What's wrong?" How long had she been awake, waiting for him?

She peered out of the window, not standing in full view of it but slightly to the side.

"Ayako?"

"I thought I saw someone from Black Hollow." She crossed her arms, biting her bottom lip. He rushed to his feet and came up behind her, both hands on her shoulders and peering past her. "They knocked on the temple door, but Cedric sent them away. I don't know what he said to them. He didn't try to wake us up."

The window opened on the courtyard and gave them a good view of the temple entrance. "When was the last time you saw them?"

She reached up and touched his hand. Some of the tension left her body. "An hour ago. They haven't been back. There were two of them. A human and an elf. I remember seeing them in the market. They were at one of the stalls. Do you think they were coming for me?"

"I wish I knew, Ayako. I don't like our odds. Maybe they were visitors? It might have nothing to do with you. How far away are we from your home?"

"Not sure. I don't even know the town we're in. We should probably ask someone. We can't be that far off track." She faced him but glanced down at her feet. "Maybe a few days?"

"We'll be okay," he tried to reassure her.

"How? We don't have any horses." She glanced up at him.

He smiled. "Do you remember the creature we rode last night? I can cast the spell again, lasts for six hours, and the beast doesn't need to rest or eat. We're going to be all right, but let's get you sorted first. If you see them, you need to point them out to me."

She nodded but kept her arms crossed, and his words hadn't done much to clear the uncertainty from her eyes. Yosef cursed under his breath; so much for being lucky Bugrush had been working with someone. The appearance of the two of them dashed his hope completely. How had they found them? He frowned, only one thing could have happened.

"What?"

"I think I know how they found us. We're going to

have to do a test."

Ayako picked up the first dress she saw. One in a vibrant shade of green with a simple cut. She donned the frock and left the changing room. The human woman behind the counter smiled brightly at her.

"It's a beautiful colour on you. Is this the one you want? Would you like me to wrap it up and have it taken to the place where you're staying?"

She shook her head. "Thank you, but I need something to wear now. My clothes were a little damaged in an attack. Is that okay?"

"Absolutely." The woman, who had introduced herself as Kinea, smiled at her brightly. She tucked a box beneath the counter.

Yosef handed her three pieces of gold for the dress and they both left.

She hadn't seen the men again, but she was pretty sure they hadn't gone far. Cedric told the men he hadn't seen Ayako or Yosef, explaining he hadn't liked the look of the two men, describing them as shifty, She made sure to thank the elderly man, but they left.

Something was preying on Yosef's mind, but he kept quiet, an usual state for him. She now knew him well enough to know when he was deep in thought. He mentioned something about a test but hadn't brought the subject up again. While they were in the clothing shop, they found out they were in the town of Breezia—a few days' travel from Dragon's Spine. If they found the sea, they could follow the coastline until they reached the Oceania city her mother originally left her in. Then one day's travel to get to the Spine.

Kinea had warned them it wasn't a safe place to visit. People had reported sightings of a black dragon circling in the sky. It darted down, vanished for a day then reappeared. No attacks had been reported, but the dragon appeared to be searching for something or someone. At least that's what people were saying. The thought sent a chill through her. Her mother might have gone searching for her and panicked when she realised her daughter wasn't there anymore.

She was going to be in a world of trouble when she arrived back at the cottage. Her mother wouldn't let her leave home ever again. Ayako let out a shuddered breath. Determined to live her life outside of the restrictions her mother set on her. She might have a talent of getting into trouble, but she'd also proven she could protect herself. Especially with her newfound abilities. And she also had the wizard; they could travel together.

If he wanted to.

152

He put a hand on her arm, and she came to a stop. "What is it?"

"They have to be tracking you somehow. A spell. Couldn't have been Bugrush, but that doesn't mean he didn't know a wizard who could infuse an item with the spell."

"Is that possible?"

Yosef cupped the back of her neck; his fingers brushed against her scales. The breath caught in her throat. He was an intensely guarded person, but another side of him came out when they were together. She couldn't have been the only one to have noticed. Had he thought about the kiss when he did things like this, or was it the furthest thing from his mind? He could completely focus on one task—an ability she envied when her thoughts were also a chaotic mess, especially around him. Except when he touched her, and everything became clear.

"Magic can do a lot of things. A wizard can do most spells. The only thing stopping them is a lack of talent."

"But there's miles between us and Black Hollow. They can track me here?" She stepped closer to him, resting her head on his shoulder. What about him inspired feelings she'd never felt before? Half the time, his attitude was terrible, cold and aloof. But that had only happened in Black Hollow. Being alone with him in a place where nobody knew who he was, he was different, almost affectionate, and it endeared him to her.

The kiss hadn't hurt, either.

He shrugged. "There is a spell to accomplish most things."

The words were almost a whisper and had tickled the small hairs near her ear. She fought the urge to sigh as the hairs on the back of her neck stood on end, her face hot, heart racing. "I haven't heard of one to track a specific part of someone, in your case, your scales. If I don't know the spell, I can't counter it. Which leaves one option. We need to keep one step ahead of them."

"How, if we don't know how they are tracking us?" She tipped her head to the side and studied the people. Humans. Gnomes. Halflings and the occasional orc. None of them appeared to be paying them any more attention than most. Some wore hooded cloaks making it next to impossible to distinguish features. Still, none of them glanced their way.

She hated being paranoid, but she also hated the idea of bringing whoever hunted her, home. Her mother could kill them in a heartbeat, but if people found out about her mother's human form, she'd be forced to either hunt them or run. Ruining her parents' lives.

"There is one more option." Yosef put his hand on her hip. "But you're not going to like it."

Ayako glanced up at him, confused. "What?"

"We kill them."

Yosef summoned the demonic steed. They couldn't risk others getting hurt, so they needed to travel by themselves. She didn't have a problem with his plan. Nobody else should get hurt because of her.

Ayako sat behind him, her arms around his waist. The steed travelled faster than a normal mount, but in the grand scheme of things, if one of the men pursuing them was a wizard, like Yosef suspected, he already had their scent. He could track them anywhere, which actually helped with Yosef's plan—find an isolated area and wait for them to appear.

"How could you be sure they'll follow?" Ayako asked.

"Doesn't matter. They either turn up or they don't. And the day ends in a fight or not."

Nerves fluttered in the pit of her stomach. She had never been in a fight before, and she had heard wizards weren't the hardiest of people. Why wasn't Yosef more nervous? He had years of experience, but, back then, he had an adventuring party with him. Now, he was by himself with a half dragon who was essentially useless until she received training. She did have a feeling he wasn't a typical wizard. There was an unwavering confidence about him. He'd come up with a plan, and he had every faith it would work out.

She couldn't tell how much time passed before he came to a halt. They disembarked, and he rubbed the snout of the steed. The beast really wasn't like anything she'd ever seen before. How could something made up of wisps of ether be solid enough to sit on? The steed vanished in a puff of purple mist.

He turned toward her, a small grin on his face. "It's going to be okay." He handed her the staff.

"Aren't you going to need this?"

He shook his head. "I'll be fine. I really need both hands for this, and you don't have a weapon."

She took the staff, the weight almost comforting. "How long do you think we have?"

"No clue. If the wizard is any good, we have a few minutes. I should be able to detect a portal." His gaze narrowed, became focused and a little scary. Ayako suffered a lot of conflicting emotions when she was near him, fear wasn't one of them. "Then I'll show you why I've got the reputation I have."

"Promise me you'll be careful?"

He touched her cheek, and she shivered, her eyes drifting closed slightly. Damn, she was falling hard. "I'll be careful. Promise me you won't do anything stupid?"

"I'll try my best."

She could feel the curve of his lips against her forehead as he kissed her. "I guess I can't ask for more."

Fear and anxiety rolled in the pit of her stomach, sickness threatening to overwhelm her. He wanted her to be brave, but easier said than done. Ayako caught the precise moment his expression changed, becoming guarded.

"Can you sense them, are they on their way?"

He nodded, grabbed her shoulders, and shoved her away. She stumbled and hit the ground, the grass doing little to cushion her fall. Yosef spun around, muttered something underneath his breath, and drew a gesture into the air. The area surrounding him pulsed with magic, whipping around him like a wind. His long dark hair flared out around him, like a living cloak. She scrambled away since she didn't want to be caught in the middle of what was about to happen. From her vantage point, she spied the blue orb growing in his palm, the way he pulled out his hands as if the energy were a piece of dough he was working.

A shadow appeared on the other side of the portal then another one. He didn't let the orb fly immediately but waited. The moment drawn out, and Ayako held her breath. He explained to her it took an enormous amount of concentration to keep hold of a spell.

The elf came through first. He wore similar robes to the clerics in the temple, even if the colours were darker and embroidered with a symbol she didn't recognize. There was the barest of warnings.

"Gentlemen." Yosef gave a brief nod in greeting before letting the spell travel on its course. The orb darted through the air with shocking speed.

The elf yelled out a warning as he drove for the left, but he wasn't fast enough. The magical energy connected with his shoulder, and he was propelled through the air, twisting before he collided with a tree. The truck cracking from the impact. She got to her feet, rushing over to the fallen body. When she was close enough, she swung the staff in a downward arc. The elf's eyes went wide before they took on a glassy stare after the sickening thud of wood against his skull.

Yosef had said he thought whoever came through the portal first would be the wizard and they needed to take him out quickly. There was a grunt of pain from behind her, and she turned in time to see Yosef spinning to the side, an arrow embedded in his shoulder, robbing him of his balance. Another arrow shot through the air as the human walked through the portal, a bow in his hand.

She screamed out a warning, and his hand shot up. Energy shimmered in front of him, and the arrow bounced off, harmless. Pure focus hardened on his features. The man smiled coldly before he turned his attention to Ayako, who still stood over the body of his comrade. He nocked another arrow, levelled the bow, and her heart practically stopped.

"Wait!"

"And give you enough time to cast another spell? I don't think so. I don't need her alive to harvest those scales." He let the arrow go.

The missile cut through the air; she couldn't even move. Time came to halt. The moment she died. She'd had her first kiss. Her first adventure. She wanted to see what the future held with Yosef. They'd never talked about the kiss...did he feel the same? Would he miss her? A few days away from home and she ended up dying. Damn, her mother was going to be angry.

Without warning, something enveloped her, and she wasn't in the same place. Frantic, she glanced around. Wasn't this where Yosef had been standing a moment ago? She glanced back at the tree and bit back another scream. The arrow had found a target, but it hadn't been her.

Yosef stumbled backwards and fell to the ground. An arrow protruded out of his leg. Fear shot through her like lightning. The contents of her stomach churned.

The mist was coming, and she did the only thing she could. Ayako ran for the man. He put out his hand, trying to stop her, but nothing would help. The acid in the pit of her stomach rolled around before shooting out of her mouth in a green toxic mist. The man screamed, trying to get away. The toxic mist enveloped him, eating away at his hand then his arm. For the briefest moment, she could make out his skeleton before the bones turned to dust.

The man ran away from her, but nothing stopped the destruction of his body. As soon as the mist reached his torso, the man let out an ear-piercing scream and fell to the ground.

The first time she'd seen the results of the acid

mist on flesh and a sickness, nothing to do with the acid breath, assaulted her. Thankfully, she missed breakfast. The incident with Bugrush in the alleyway? She barely remembered anything but the smell. This moment, however, had been etched into her memory. Her stomach twisted itself into knots, and when the screaming finally stopped, she collapsed to the ground. Exhausted.

Yosef crawled to her. "Are you okay?"

She nodded, trying not to take in the sight of the remains of the human in front of her.

Chapter Fifteen

There weren't many things he missed about being an adventurer. He could count them on one hand, but being shot wasn't one of them. The arrow in his shoulder sent ripples of pain down his arm, making the tips of his fingers go numb. She was hesitant to touch it, but the blasted thing couldn't stay in his shoulder. The wound needed pressure to stop the bleeding. He didn't think the archer had hit anything vital, but the pain still brought tears to his eyes.

Ayako helped him snap the arrow and pull the shaft out the back then she dressed the wound with the extra bandages he'd bought from the clerics.

The injury to his thigh worried him more. After removing the arrow, he cast burning hands and cauterized the wound. She gave him a twig to bite, but the gasp of pain escaped him before he could stop it. Her eyes were wide, her hands hesitant.

"Believe me, I've lived through worse."

"Have you?" She sounded doubtful.

When he finished dressing his wounds, she helped him to his feet, his arm on her shoulder, the staff in his free hand. "I've been swallowed by a Lying Lily, a big carnivorous plant found in forest areas. We encountered the carnivorous plant in the Weeping Woods whilst we were hunting ghosts. The petals are laid out on the forest floor and when an unwary traveller steps in the centre of them, the petals close up, sealing the traveller inside."

"What was it like?"

"Smelly."

She laughed.

"I kid you not. That plant must have killed quite a few people who ended up in its clutches. It dissolves bodies until they're a slushy gloop it can digest. The smell was terrible."

"How did you get out?"

"A fire spell I keep prepared in cases of emergency. The party was trying their hardest to break through the petals to get me out, but Gru told me they were like steel. Nothing cut through them. I figured the lily's defences might only extend to the outside. So, I cast the spell and burnt a hole right through."

Tension left her, and he swore she smiled. Killing the archer would probably weigh on her mind a lot—even more than Bugrush—but this time, the toxic mist had been a deliberate choice and not a reflex to protect herself. Best to change the topic. "About the kiss."

She stiffened, and he blamed his poor social skills for not being able to bring up the subject more tactfully.

"I was wondering if we were going to talk about it," she murmured.

"I can only summon the demonic steed once a day, I need to rest before I can cast again. This is as good a time as any to talk about it."

Ayako covered his hand with hers. She was smaller than him, but she had a strength to her he hadn't acknowledged before. Only a week had passed. How could she have upended his life so completely in such a short amount of time? What she'd lived through proved she wasn't a damsel in distress. She was selfless. Braver than she knew. Why was he surprised he was falling in love with her?

"Yosef?"

He laughed. "I meant it. The kiss. A little caught up in the heat of the moment, I know. I've been fighting the urge for a while and then I thought I'd lost you."

She bit her bottom lip and glanced around the forest.

"What's wrong?" He frowned. Had he

misinterpreted her reaction to him? "I apologise if I overstepped my mark..."

"I think someone is scrying on me."

They came to a stop.

"Any ideas to who it might be?" Did the group of men have a boss, someone in charge who pulled the strings? Yosef had checked the wizard's body before they left. He had hit the tree with such force, the impact had broken his neck, more likely then him dying from the blow by Ayako. So, he couldn't have been doing the scrying.

"I have an idea. I don't know what I prefer though." She didn't elaborate, except to say she didn't think the person meant her any harm.

They walked for a little bit. Yosef glanced across at Ayako. She hadn't acknowledged his comments about their kiss. Maybe she didn't feel the same way? He had his problems—poor social skills and a general dislike of people. She was his opposite. They shouldn't work.

"I could have taken the hit."

Her words made him frown. "What do you mean?"

"I'm sure the arrow wouldn't have killed me. I've already healed the spider stab wound. You didn't have to swap our positions."

"The arrow didn't kill me, either. I acted on

instinct, and I would do it again in a heartbeat." He squeezed her shoulder. "Consider us even. You saved my life, and I've saved yours."

"You could have died." Her eyes shimmered with tears; they trickled down her face, leaving a wet path in their wake.

He stopped and turned her to face him, but her eyes were downcast. He gently raised her face only to find tears there, her eyes bottomless emerald pools. "But I didn't die."

"But you could have."

"But I didn't." He brought his lips down on hers, ignoring the flash of pain from his shoulder. "I might whistle if air catches me in the right direction," he whispered against her lips then wiped away her tears before kissing her again. The tension left her body as she put her arms around his shoulders, holding him closer. Yosef flinched as she knocked the wound, and she made to pull away. He didn't let her. "I think I can stand a little more pain."

"Then I think you should kiss me again."

Epilogue

He held her hand as they walked towards the small cottage in Dragon's Spine, their fingers intertwined. They had stopped at the seaside town for a few days, letting him heal up. Even from their current distance away, he spied a woman in the garden. The skirt of her dress and the strands of her long black hair caught in the wind. A man sat on the steps leading up to the cottage.

As soon as the woman caught sight of them, she ran in their direction. The black dress melted away, and giant wings sprouted out of her back. He caught the precise moment Ayako's face turned white as if all the blood had left her. "She isn't going to try and attack me, is she?"

"She might be a little overprotective." She took off in a run of her own, waving her hands, trying to get her mother's attention. "Mother, you need to calm down."

The black dragon circled above them then dove down. Yosef quickly conjured a portal and vanished, reappearing near the cottage. A quaint little building with steps leading up to the front door and a garden full of wildflowers. The man who sat on the steps, Ayako's father, nodded at him.

"Afternoon."

"Afternoon. Any way to stop your wife from eating me?"

He shrugged. "She's always been a little protective of our daughter. A little impulsive and worry about the consequences later, kind of lady. You brought her home safely, you have my appreciation. What's your name, boy?"

"Yosef." He bristled slightly, a memory of Grogswald addressing him the same way.

The dragon shifted into human form, stalking towards them. Ayako was still a little way behind her, but she was running, trying to close the distance.

"Nice to meet you. I'm Tomas, and the woman coming at us with murder in mind is Beltrix. I hope you'll be joining us for tea...I mean, if you survive."

"Why are you with my daughter?" Beltrix's face was covered in cracked skin; wisps of smoke came from them. Her eyes were red.

"Helping her get home." He raised his hands and eased away from her. "There is no need for us to fight."

"Then you can leave."

"Mother, stop. This is Yosef." Ayako stepped

between them. "Is this really the first encounter you want to have with my family?" she said to him who smiled.

He was sure he could beat the dragon; he had at least one spell that would knock her out. But...she was right. Probably not a good first impression to make on her family. Instead, he grabbed her hand then leaned down to brush a kiss across her cheek. "You're right. You have my sincerest apologies."

Beltrix scowled at him, but he ignored her.

"It's nice to meet Ayako's family. Your daughter and I have had quite the trip to get to you."

Tomas stood, brushed dirt off his trousers then held out his hand to shake. Yosef accepting. "Welcome to our home. A friend of our daughter is more than welcomed here. Isn't that right, Beltrix?" He nudged his wife in the side who growled at him before something like a grimace crossed her face.

"Absolutely. Let's get inside, and I'll make us all something to drink," she said through gritted teeth.

Ayako led him up the steps and inside the cottage. Yosef caught the tail end of the conversation between wife and husband, mother and father.

"She came back with a man. She was only gone for a week."

The Wizard of Black Hollow

"You always said you wanted her to find someone."

"But in a week?" she hissed. "And a wizard of all people. Those people always attract trouble."

"A powerful one as well. Did you see how quickly he conjured the portal?" Tomas chuckled. "Impressive. She seems quite taken with him, and him, her. You can't protect her all the time. All you'll end up doing is pushing her away."

Beltrix the Black sighed. "Gods, I hate when you're right."

"You love me really." The man who'd been brave enough to fall in love with a dragon chuckled.

"Idiot, but I can eat him if it all goes wrong, right?"

"Of course, sweetheart, but let's get to know him first."

Thank you for reading The Wizard of Black Hollow. Next in Series is